From The Ashes

Writing on the Wall
Toxteth Library
Windsor Street, Liverpool
L8 1XF

Published by Writing on the Wall, 2023

© Remains with the authors

Design and Layout by Jenny Dalton
Cover Design by Po.Ke Marketing

978-1-916571-02-0

All rights reserved. No part of this publication may be reproduced, stored in a retrieval system, or transmitted, in any form or by any means, electronic, mechanical, photocopying, recording or otherwise, without the prior permission of the publishers.

0151 703 0020
info@writingonthewall.org.uk
www.writingonthewall.org.uk

Content Warning:

This book contains strong language, sexual references, mentions of death, violence, abuse, grief, substance abuse, infant mortality and trichotillomania.

Table of Contents

Foreword — i
Blue Saint

Introduction — iii
Helen Jeffery

Ollie Adebisi	1
Michael Ananins	10
Artemis Arches	14
Leonisha Barley	20
David Bourne	30
Delia Campbell	32
Oliver Catherall	37
Amesbury Clarke	48
Joseph Clift	58
Dominic Connolly	67
Garry Connolly	71
Peter Cousins	82
Steve Connolly	89
Maisy Gordon	96
Angela Grant	103
James M. Greilley	106
Siobhan Harte	113
Sharon Harte	120
Iain Hendrie	123
Jennifer Hughes	124
Michael Inniss	128

Caitlyn Jones	140
John Kelly	148
Rikki Kielle	149
Anne Lunt	151
Matthew Lunt	153
Jennifer McAlister	154
Lucy McAllister	163
Jacqueline McKenzie	166
David McLintock	175
Fergus Michaelson	181
Mandy Morgan	183
Sarah Murray	193
Hana Musimurimwa	201
Rachel Naomi	212
C.D Phillip	221
Amanda Pinnington	228
Tashi Thornley	236
Vincent Quirk	247
Gerard Sheridan	256
Ian Tudor	259
Keith Anthony Vaughan	266

Afterword 267
Madeline Heneghan and Mike Morris

Foreword

Welcome to this wonderful anthology – a collection that reflects the incredible journey that was undertook together in the realm of creative exploration and self-discovery during the Write to Work course. As a facilitator, I was privileged to witness the transformative power of words, guiding a diverse group from aspiring writers to confident storytellers.

Teaching on the course was so heartwarming and rewarding; it was an immersion into the hearts and minds of individuals that had compelling stories to tell, beautiful stories that fiercely bubbled beneath the surface, waiting to be expressed. Witnessing their evolution, not just as writers but as individuals embracing and fully delving into their creative identity, was awe-inspiring. This anthology is a testament to their journey – a journey of therapeutic expression and the joy of discovering the significance of their voices.

Write to Work provides a crucial platform for individuals to realise the therapeutic power of writing. For those initially hesitant, putting pen to paper becomes a cathartic release and a source of genuine joy. The stories within these pages capture the profound transformations of each participant beyond mere words.

It is incredibly important that writers are brought together as it creates a natural, nurturing environment that causes communities to flourish, which in turn, provides a launching pad for creativity.

I hope that these pages inspire and serve as a reminder that, within the written word, we discover not only our stories' richness but also the limitless potential for growth and connection.

Blue Saint
Multi-Disciplinary Artist, Writer & Write to Work Tutor

Introduction

Following the launch of our first compendium *Beyond the Storm* in August 2023, we are delighted to bring you *From the Ashes*. This second collection brings together new voices from across the Liverpool City Region, created through Writing on the Wall's longest-running professional development course, Write to Work. The writers whose work is contained within this book come from across several courses and their work spans many themes including: identity, love, childhood, motherhood, growing up and growing old, as well as what it means to be defined by race or disability and constrained by gender.

As a recent addition to Writing on the Wall and Project Manager for Write to Work since March 2023, I was delighted when Jenny invited me to write the introduction to this compendium. I was also hoping that I might be successful in pitching a suitable title but alas, it was not meant to be! That honour fell to one of WoW's newest members of staff, Caroline, for her suggestion, 'From the Ashes', which was met with a resounding 'YES' from the WoW team. As you read through the prose, script and verse contained in these pages I think you will understand why it is such a fitting title. There are stories wrapped up within the realms of myth and legend, fantasy and fiction, some asking questions in a world where there are no answers. Yet despite the difficulties and trauma evident within some of the writing, there is also humour, strength, resilience, love and hope. A sense of new beginnings forged from the ashes of the past.

Please be aware that this book contains strong language, sexual references, mentions of death, violence, abuse, grief, substance abuse, infant mortality and trichotillomania. If this is not something you can read right now, we completely understand – your mental health matters.

Thank you to all the inspirational tutors who dedicated their time to Write to Work throughout this course: your skills, warmth and depth of experience bring something special to the course and its participants.

Thank you to the whole WoW staff team who contribute to Write to Work, but a special mention to my right-hand woman, Project Worker Talisha Thomas-Lindsay for her continuous hard work. Heartfelt thanks also to former WoW staff Amy Carrington and Naomi Scott, to our Publishing Coordinator Jenny for her endless patience and hard work, and to our talented designers at Po.Ke Marketing for the fantastic cover design.

Writing on the Wall is part of the Directions project in partnership with The Women's Organisation and is part funded by the European Social Fund. We would like to thank our funders for making the project and this incredible compendium possible.

Our final and most important thanks go to the writers of *From the Ashes*. Thank you for sharing your writing with us every week during the workshops and congratulations on being published authors! Thank you for writing this book, thank you for reminding us that, much like the legendary phoenix, we are strong enough to rise from the ashes with determination in the face of difficulty.

Whether you've risen once or a thousand times before,
You have the strength to do it once more.
Tashi Thornley – Write to Work

Helen Jeffery
Write to Work Project Manager, Writing on the Wall

In A Name
Ollie Adebisi

What's in your name?
Yourba, Arabic
But quick
– what does it really mean?
'Wealth fits me.'
That's exotic, pretty.
Except when it's not:
A tired teacher lifts her pen
'Can you just spell that unusual name for me again?'
When TV's flicker on, enunciating terrorist –
'Miss, why did people that look like Yemi do this?'
Both spoke with a closed fist.

What's in your name?
I never met the man who chose it,
he never knew if it fit.
Where are you from?
A little place far away…Coventry –
but, where are you *really* from?
Manchester. You wouldn't know it hearing me.
I'm not trying to be funny –
Neither am I.
Can I touch your hair?
If you want vodka in your eye.

That's aggressive. Don't blame me, it's just so lovely.
I won't blame you –
but I'm gonna do
what I have to do.

Who Put Bella In the Wych Elm?
Ollie Adebisi

I grew tired of them quickly that night and plotted our escape.
The ale soured before it had even touched
my lipstick.
Stop!
Your hand soared away back to your wine.
It knew better than to touch me in the lamp light again.
Stop!
Her smile burst across my defences.
I braided her fingers in mine and our heels clicked away
from cigarette smoke.
Quickly!
Before we felt the shadows.
Before we felt the cold of our wedding rings.

On the field our bodies rained on the grass.
Her breath was an atmosphere I thrived in,
drinked in,
sinked
in.

She suffocated my common sense like thick wool.
I was sure we had convinced them.
Home early to slave away!

Making sure everything was ready for:
Our. Men.
We surrendered our bodies ritually.
Inside and out.

Our flesh finally belonged to us that night.

The bark is my halo now, my home.
My scream refracted through her as she watched, a siren –
stop.
Let me think of following her laugh through endless corridors,
both snug in clouds of perfume.
Safe.
A beginning every time we met.

Chalk Sugar Cigarette
Ollie Adebisi

Rorschach period stain.
Why did you have to show your ink in here?
I'm ten
and I don't think I'll ever be little again.

I tried to find the source:
a cut, another reason.
But no luck!
I'm leaking colourful treason.

I am doomed to feel:
the stab / weight / ache.

The feeling of my sister
throwing a twenty pack
of sanny pads at my head.
Her dealing
with an alien in her midst
who looked like she'd shat the bed.

School said it's part of becoming
A WOMAN.
Lazy lead legs from morning play pretzeled
in lines, floor wooden.

BOY / GIRL / BOY / GIRL.

Benny croaked out the word 'penis'
acted like he thought it was just for piss.
As if!
I saw him chase Alice
pin her down,
ignore our small voices…
her frown.

My organs are sacrificed
for some far-off foetus that
might grow / live / die.
Why should my clumsy body suffer now
when I still make
pictures
out of the sky?

God
Ollie Adebisi

Skin to skin, his lips crushed against my forehead,
insulating my warmth
against the winters.

Mind to mind, smiling with teeth sweetly
he burrowed into my skull.
his rules gifted summers.

Laughing at my sobs,
he angled my chin to sink my tears into the pavements
whilst I mouthed prayer.

His gaze was protection for a time.
but like everything in that binary world, a lie.
still I spoke to him, staring into coarse fibres.
careful never to raise my voice, knees burning as I knelt.
it was his house after all.
willing for whispers: I starved myself to feel closer to him.
my hollow stomach birthed emptiness.

actually –
come.
pull on my boots and run through my duality.

is it comfortable cloaking yourself in my fantasy?
I'm watching you through gilded gauze as you dance
in my costume.
learning the way the bodies moved around me.
climbing out of yourself.
can you taste the filth? can you feel the shame?
let me teach you how to hide from him.
how to pretend to forget.

I realised later I'd mistook beauty for pattern, flattened
my own criticism.
I crafted meaning meticulously, desperately.
I saw snow but I always smelled ash.
without him to envelop me I looked to the moon.
she cradled me.

still, my pain
MY GOD – breathed to me in the night:
'do you want to sit next to me?'
the addiction, affliction of him guided me to my seat.
I dug my nails into my skin to tolerate it all but
my
flesh
felt
so
shallow.

From the Ashes

I felt too small.

I fell asleep and woke up to the streetlights on his lap once.
his home was
home is never where we ended up.
the silhouettes conquered the evening;
the perfume of petrichor cloyed.
the radio was a small voice
yearning
a sea of static.

I scratched at my neck to near decapitation
whilst I explained my existence to him.

the frame rate slowed to tableau.

he was never listening.

Thatcher
Michael Ananins

You finally have it all
You've taken all that you stole
You ripped the hearts from the poor
and left them in a hole
You've killed off northern industry
and raped the national health
Now you sit in your Downing Street Palace
and wallow in your wealth
You would be queen of Europe
If you could only steal a throne
Well, the only thing you haven't done
is steal blood from a stone
Oh, you proved you're stubborn and strong
Prime example, the Falklands war
You stole the lives of hundreds
You dirty, fucking whore
Lorenzo, the Argentinian was only seventeen
English Tommy a few years more
They'll never see their Mum's again
You dirty. Fucking. Whore.
But it's us, the people, who give you the power
To fill a grave with a mother's baby
Maybe, one day, a rebel's bullet will get you
The Iron Lady.

Pen Man
Michael Ananins

My name is Mark, but everyone in work calls me Pen Man. Basically, because I always have four or five pens in my shirt pocket. I work twelve, sometimes fifteen hour shifts on a psychiatric ward, and I really just don't care.

I don't care about a lot of things. Especially cheap talk. The kind of chatter that is required for general politeness. In fact, I dislike it so much that on my days off I'd take a bus to somewhere I'm not familiar with then go on a nice long walk with no need for polite chatter.

Last Wednesday was different though. I took a bus to an affluent part of town and began my peaceful stroll. It wasn't long before I was completely lost, both on this journey and my ever decreasing life.

I can almost hear my father now, 'Why don't you get a mobile phone? One with GPS? I've said it many times. Get yourself a phone.'

Yes, but then I wouldn't be able to do what I'm doing now. Get lost, away from everyone.

I quickly came to the awful realisation that I would have to ask someone for directions. The area was posh. Tree lined with large, detached houses. I bit the bullet and strolled up the large driveway of the first house. I soon noticed that the house had lots of bunting around the windows and a banner over the door that I thought said *Happy Birthday,* but as I got closer I saw it actually said *Happy Funday.*

I sarcastically muttered to myself, 'Ooh, look. Someone's having fun, but why no balloons?'

Before I could ring the bell, the door flew open and a middle-aged woman appeared with a big smile on her face.

'Are you the clown?' she shrieked. 'Oh, please tell me you're here to entertain the children. We've been waiting such a long time!'

Now, twenty years ago, when I had a sense of fun, I would have said, 'Yes, I'm Mr Bubbles! Sorry, I don't look much like a clown but I was just mugged and they took away my big shoes and water firing lapel flower!'

But before I could say anything, she grabbed my arm and pulled me into the house. She shouted over her shoulder, 'He's here! The clown is here!'

I thought to myself, 'If only she knew how wrong, or maybe how right, she was.

I was pulled straight into the living room where I was greeted by 'the children.' There was an overweight 'child' dressed in an ill-fitting Victorian sailor suit. Two girls in identical pink dresses and Easter bonnets, both licking giant lollipops. Another boy was dressed in a 1950's style Just-William school uniform. They all froze and stared at me.

After a few seconds, they all quietly said, 'Clown.'

If that wasn't strange enough, none of them were actually children. They were all in their mid-to-late eighties.

Noticing the pens in my pocket, the sailor 'boy' shouted, 'Pen Man!'

'Maybe they're prizes?' said the schoolboy.

I was horrified. Both staff and patients at work call me Pen Man. They couldn't possibly know this. Maybe it's just an obvious thing. I have pens, therefore I am Pen Man!

I started to think that somewhere along my journey today I was involved in a fatal accident in which I died, and this before me is my punishment for being a miserable Pen Man. An eternal funday with these fun seeking people.

And, of course, I was the clown.

Oar
Artemis Archer

Her sorrow and her joy
weaved with all that lies between
A tapestry that holds me in open arms
Etchings upon our bodies
Initials carved into the curves of our songs
Mining depths with caressing syncopation,
earth loosens
Whilst from above,
raindrops fall upon canvas
Rains upon home
White noise that calms the head storm
guiding her in
She picks up the oar and we row
Sometimes in turn,
sometimes as one intimate rhythm that shifts,
changes course, lifts and drops again, drops
Nothing spoken
Exquisite corpse melodies
Delicate fibres that become threads
that become rope
that become seamless
Her songstress, me strings
whispering the future
to tentative fingers

coaxing their deliberate touch
She sings memories and imaginings
An ancestral eye reading the sacred river
that carries her own dreaming
from source to the sea.

Blue Ray
Artemis Archer

Songbirds perch upon the midline of time
and begin to nest in the lining of my heart
The regularity of its beating a rhythmic foundation
for the intricate compositions of
gentle determination, coloured yarn and twig
The staccato of feathered hops and
stretched vibratos call me to full presence
And from all the spaces and places I have been, I return
Gathering in the pieces of what is mine to keep
I smooth down my dress and become a song
Composed by my own birds
A blue ray and a charm of gold
It's an unfamiliar sonic landscape into braided melodies
Stirred, the oak trees unfurl their green
Becoming shade for the heat yet to come.

Divine Surrender in Pink Neon
Artemis Archer

Jesus is in bronze surrender
As the chaplain
attends those
who come here to pray
It is their stillness in sitting, she says,
that gives them away.

Clutch
Artemis Archer

A clutch of untended brokenness
In the backyard of pieces
Still clinging on years later
So much so, it's hard to shake off
Though it remains possible
Heaviness shuffles, moving pots around,
then sweeping up all the eggshells
They'll soon be turned into dust and mixed in with the soil
From cracked dismemberment to uncountable
Like a body turned to ash white as snowdrop
It's difficult to imagine, but from that soil
sunflowers will grow.

Gravity is Dissolving
Artemis Archer

To cross the bridge is a choice
Spinning with the outer planets to
the sound of waxing; a crescent earth merges with
Venus at one o'clock
There, the water beneath you stills,
and you see yourself again
Two stones hit the surface and become eyes; radiating
circles calling to that not yet perceived
You were there and now you're not
You have free will, and your blood is yours to spill
Stone gods remove their masks
Motherless strangers never stated,
relentless in their masochism,
throw themselves at walls again and again
And all the while, truth is connected by a silver thread
from the crystalised iron core, to the source o fall that is
With a quality both fragile and robust
Untether now; gravity is dissolving
You know it, you fly in your sleep
Remember the weightlessness
Soaring up; a heightened flight of possibility,
that knows the rich dark of soil where earthworms
dwell
Droughts come and go

With strong faith, vision like an eagle
reworks and untangles dreams
It is the vixen's obligation to guard
With one ear cocked, she protects
and abandons in spirals
Feel into the drum of your belly and watch as rare flowers begin to grow under you
Whilst in the night's sky, new stars appear with each step you take.

The Little White Van
Leonisha Barley

Driving down Harlow Street I can see,
The Little White Van, across the River Mersey.
What could it be up to? I wonder
Who's in that van? A baker, a banker, a delivery driver?

Across Grafton and down Park Street,
If he was delivering me a parcel, who would I meet?
But who delivers in a Little White Van?
Everyone knows they're driven by the scary man.

I love seeing the water and the boats along Sefton Street.
If he drove through the tunnel, I wonder who I'd meet?
Maybe a giant who escaped his captives by the skin of his enormous feet.
The Little White Van was the first thing he saw and in he leapt.
Well not quite leapt – 'Oh no, I don't fit. They're going to catch me,' he wept.
Some little kids were around and told him, 'Do not fret.'
1, 2, 3 they shoved his back and, in his body, went.
HOORAYY!! they shouted.
But it wasn't quite the celebration they'd hoped for,
Because now his lanky legs were sticking out the passenger door!

Drive down Harlow Street, nice and slow.
Let the thoughts in your mind flow.
In your imagination, what places will The Little White Van go?
Create a post with the hashtag #thelittlewhitevan
I can't wait to read where your van goes: France, Mexico, Sudan, Japan?

Freaky Farting Frogs From Finland
Leonisha Barley

Fatima's family- Femi's family friends.
Freddy - Femi's friend.
Femi's formal family function.
Frocks, **food,** frills!

Freckled Freddy fancies Friendly Fatima.
Friendly Fatima fancies Fat Femi.
Friendship formed from favourite food - fufu!
Femi, Fatima- fufu fanatics!
French fries -Freddy's fav feast.

Fury filled, Freddy found freaky farting frogs from Finland.
Freddy filled Femi's fridge full.
Feeling famished Fat Femi finds fridge.

FAECES!

Fat, farting frogs fly from Femi's fridge!
Farting frogs: Fly, Flip, **FLOP**, *Flick,* Flood food.
Frightening Fatima's family.

Femi forewarns: 'FOOD FIGHTTTTTT !!!!!'
Food - Flys, Flips, **FLOPS**, *Flicks,* Floods Femi's family function.

Femi's father, Fredrick, frowned furiously, faulting Femi.
Freddy felt fulfilment framing Femi for farting frogs fiasco.
Freddy fetched five frogs freeing Fatima's family from fright,
Furthermore, forecasting Fatima falls for Fred.

Fortunately, Freddy's formulated farting frogs failed.
For, fear- free Fatima found flying farting frogs fantastically funny,
Feeling further fondness for Femi.
Flabbergasted Freddy fessed.
Femi forgave Freddy for framing.
Femi, Fatima, Freddy fabricated forever friendships formed from favourite fellows- **Freaky Farting Frogs from Finland!**

I Wish
Leonisha Barley

I wish I didn't have to manipulate my shrunken 4C hair into styles disguised as protective,
In order to come across as the type of black girl that in society is respected.

I wish I didn't have to go through the office Q&A,
When I go into work with a new hairstyle on a Monday.

I wish I didn't have to think twice before I put on a short skirt,
because if anything happened I'd be blamed for being a flirt.

I wish women didn't have to go through so much pain, and that black women weren't 3x more likely to die in childbirth because they're ignored when they try to explain.

I wish I didn't have to live under a ticking clock of time pressure,
Because if I leave it too late, my eggs will expire.

I wish money could be distributed evenly in every part

of the world,
in every country, throughout every part of society.
Because if that was so people won't feel the need to leave their beautiful lands in search of safety or opportunity.

I wish I didn't have to look over my shoulder as I walk alone from a day out in the park,
because nowadays you can't even trust a police officer who offers to give you a lift after dark.

I wish everyone had the confidence to go out there and slay;
regardless of what ignorant people have to say!

I wish tall women could strut their stuff in heels that make them as high as a skyscraper;
while men secure in their masculinity hail words of adoration towards her.

I wish I could stomp out everything that lowers a woman's self-esteem underneath my platformed shoe,
because just for being a woman in this world- **We deserve to be looked up to!**

More wishes I'm sure I gather as I travel the world and grow

But for now, I stand in my skyscraper heels, throw my wishes up to the sky
and I let them go!

50 Soda Bottles Underneath the Bed
Leonisha Barley

Joe:

Living with sickle cell hurt like hell.
In other countries like England, they put people in sickle cell crisis on morphine.
And did you know by age 8, many children with SCD have had to remove their spleen!
At least that didn't happen to me.
They said they bought me here so I could be pain free.

This being dead thing ain't so bad, at least I avoided a big whopping,
I used to steal bottles of soda from the bar when no one was looking.
I used to count them as I hid them under my bed, I counted 50 on my last night.
Vimto, Fanta and my favourite Sprite!
I know now that I should have drank water and soft drinks made it worse,
But I had to find some way to stop the constant thirst.

Apparently, I've had it since I was born but the doctor never told my mum or dad,

And when I think about that, it makes me feel actually really sad.
Because I'm going to miss them and all my brothers and sisters
I've asked to stay a little longer. For now, I'm one of 'The Drifters!'

I get to visit my family and sometimes I go and see my best friend Saliatu,
I hear them having conversations about me. I miss them and they miss me too.
Mums don't go to their children's funerals in our culture. It's too much to take.
But my big sis stood in for her at the church, to help with the heart break.
Mum looks different, not so big and fluffy.
She cries a lot now cause she's really sad
and dad acts busy and is always mad.
So, when I visit I play the piano for them to make them happy.
Dad taught me to play when I was 9,
I remember him saying "a go teach you ow for play di piano fine."
He didn't know I was only going to be here for a short amount of time.

But I guess all that practice paid off,

Cause now I'm a ghost ... whooo..ooo and when I play the piano my sisters scream.
It's really fun spooking people out. I like being part of 'The Drifter Kidz' team.

But they say my time as a drifter is almost over,
and that it's nearly time to let go forever.
But I don't mind because guess what
I'm gonna get to fly!
I can't wait to be able to watch my family, like a movie, from way up high.
I'm gonna be just like the beautiful birds I used to watch, flying up in the sky.

Griffy's Song
David Bourne

High and low, up and down.
I don't know where to go.
It's not the world of playing out anymore.
This world isn't kind and it's not so pure
The smoke I breathe clouds my vision,
There are things about me, I want to be unwritten.
Had some nice friends, they were alright
But we got into a fight
Now I'm all alone, but it's OK, it's gonna be alright
Up and down, high and low
I don't know where to go.

Put A Little Joy In Heart
David Bourne

Every day when I look in the mirror
I see new grey hair and a wrinkle line
I know one day soon the pain will stop
Just be happy with what you got
Put a little joy in your heart
Put a little joy in your soul
Every day I hear a new sad story
And I see another broken soul
Don't worry about tomorrow.
Just live for the here and now
Put a little
Everyday life is too precious to waste,
On all the bad that puts you down
Just put feelings aside now.
Just be glad you're alive.
Put a little joy.

Listening
Delia Campbell

'You're mental,' they say.

I laugh along and smile. If only they knew they were talking to another person – being me – we have 'dark days,' and 'hard times.' That isn't depression.

Depression is very dark and you fight with yourself constantly until you can reach a 'peace agreement.' They come in a box from the pharmacy and you take them to reduce the bad feelings and thoughts that you live with every day.

Oh my quiet mind, what has happened? Why are we not debating things? Please don't leave me as I don't know how to cope with the deafening quiet. This is a strange numb feeling you have, you start to disassociate yourself with people and things…start to become a version of someone else living in you.

'Cry,' 'talk,' 'let it out,' people say. But they don't want to really hear you.

Listening is an art and to perfect it you need practice and to learn that you're not the only 'mental' one is weird. Somewhere in the dark you'll find a 'tool' to open your mouth and small things come out, and as you practice with this 'tool,' you'll create, and look after the tool to make it work well for you, then you start

mining and in a blip, you find the light.
Wonderful
Delia Campbell

When you were born into this world,
I instantly adored you.
I watched you sleep,
taste your first foods,
watched your first steps.

I watched you grow
and smile,
to see how amazing you are
and are going to be.

You cannot see yourself
through my eyes
but if you did
you would see truly
how wonderful you are.

Ride On
Delia Campbell

What does the black sheep do to be different?
I suppose the colour could change
but it is still the same sheep.
I'm proud to be the black sheep
in my maternal family
as I change my hair colour
and will not abide by things
that my family expect
I will be me!

So, when you see a black sheep on its own
cheer it!
As it is unique,
strong,
resilient
and brave.

Walking
Delia Campbell

The full moon glowed as I put my trainers on and went for a walk along the front. Having the sea and smelling the saltiness in the air is so refreshing and soul soothing. The moon is a recharge for me. It is happiness, quiet, calm, and exciting. I love feeling like this. I am alive and living my best life, right this moment. I never want it to stop.

When I get back home, I am at peace. Everything and everyone and feeling joyful and grateful for being able to do this and experience it.

I go to sleep, and wake up feeling refreshed and ready for anything, for whatever the day has in store.

I feel alive. Ready! Keys, phone, bag. Let's go. Tram to work today so I can read my book and I might grab a cuppa on the way.

It gives me an exciting feeling. It gives me hope.

I'm home again when I smell cakes, sweets, and a lovely candle going.

Grades
Delia Campbell

Clearing the sink for the fifth time, her eyes filled with tears. She bit her lip as she tried to keep it together. She was proud of me! I finally got it, the results I needed.

'Yippee,' I shouted, and went running towards her and she turned and hugged me tight.

Mum and daughter strike again. Mum was always my strength, if only she knew it, and was also my cheerleader and critic too.

'I'm going to be a nurse!' I shout.

She smiles and laughs, 'Yes you are, I knew you could do it!'

Tears of a Raven King
Oliver Catherall

The Gods had blessed Brýnan Ri Bannau, the High King, King of the peaks with a kingdom and fortune that would evoke a fierce envy from any man. But now, sat high upon his throne, a sadness bereft the King.

Far from the warmth of his true love, the many winters he had lived began to show, the cross hatched lines on his palms were more worn with each day's passing away from his adopted home on the lake, its magic, and the love he bore for its lady, Mereá who had rescued him from an ill fate all to certain in his youth. He would recall her beauty and how every day on the cusp of dawn, as the first light would swing through the trees, she would kneel beside the lake, her long, auburn hair curled to meet its reflection, and would still the very tide and begin to sing her sweet gentle song that would lay upon the water like an early morning mist, awakening all in her realm.

For a brief, lingering moment, he would find peace, back in her embrace only for it to fade into a distant memory of a lifetime long gone, but one still gripped to Brýnan's heart. It no longer shielded him from the plagues of time for it was her magic that had allowed Brýnan and their two sons to live the span of many lives, safe inside her kingdom.

Now, like all things, it began to creep up swiftly ageing him from a young man to one facing the twilight of his days, with the encroaching years trespassing upon his person. A field of grey now weaved its way into his black hair and the weight of rule had amassed a tapestry of wrinkles on his once handsome face. The unmerciful tax of time was cruel and unyielding; his strength famed throughout the land had left him and he ached to feel the power of his youth once again.

It brought joy to his ever-faithful Faistines, the three mysterious ravens, his own personal soothsayers who had been biding their time for mischief, waiting for the smallest weakness in his character that they could use to their own means.

'Revered as a God, aged like a man,' they squawked, flapping around, their words sniggering at him, one by one chanting the same thing.

He was no fool. He knew the ravens, their jet-black feathers rang out a greenish-blue in the candle lights of his great hall. They were up to some mischief. True, they had always followed him like a shadow, clinging closer than kin, helping mostly for what was their own gains, but what those gains were eluded Brýnan. The promise of a remedy from his affliction of age fooled him against his better judgement.

The golden chalice that he drank from, a gift given

from the Gods as an aid in the fight against the darkness and its legions gave the bearer the strength of ten men whenever used, but it did not pause the woes of time. It was a gift most treasured amongst his people, such a thing of beauty that only the bravest among his kin wielded it. As the chalice passed from one chief's hands to another it grew as more legends and tales were added, each panel depicted a hero or feat against the Goddess Torcrá and her tormented crusade to destroy all life in this world. There were the exploits of Broinn the Mighty who killed the Goddess' champion in hand-to-hand combat that lasted many days, so long in fact that it is said his last strike upon the beast changed the season to the next. Another saw the fleeing of their people by the Great Queen Brigit who saved them from the crashing of the great sea wall that brought an end to the first age of light. Each part a fitting testimony to the lineage of Llyr and an agonising reminder of epic tales achieved by his kin.

Still to this day honoured, quite rightly, by their descendants to such an envy of Brýnan that he ached for such fame. As the sands of time trickled on, he sensed his adventure was soon coming to an end and he questioned whether his deeds would be worthy of such fitting remembrance.

He spent countless hours hidden under the last flickering light. The fading candles and their broken embers clinging onto the dying solitary wick as it battled the ever-looming darkness that dwarfed his quarters, whilst Brýnan disguised as a philosopher as he pondered the rhetoric.

Now all he had was the unanswered riddles in the dark, would the saga's recount his deeds? Would the bards sing of his enemies' sorrow long after Brýnan had departed for the next world? Or would he simply slip into the forgotten? Would the flowers left on his tomb be left to weed only for one day to be mistaken for nothing more than a lonely mound upon the earth? He knew to triumph in the saga's was to triumph over death itself.

Such a weight sat heavy upon his brow and this was all too easily noticed by the raven's. They used his desperation to coax Brýnan to new heights of lunacy. As his obsession grew, so did the obscure remedies. He bought clothes and creams lathered with magic and mystics and scholars were used to create all kinds of frilly, interesting inventions to try and reverse the effects of his grizzled appearance. He even banned mirrors in the royal hall and anything that could conceive a reflection for fear of seeing his own. The ravens, with their yellow beady eyes, watched on and fluffed their black feathers, patiently biding their time.

The days grew longer, fresh flowers adorned the

kingdom and a time of celebration dawned on the morrow. None were privy to the changes in Brýnan, the High King, except for a select few, sworn to a burdened secrecy. His temper was shorter than before and for all the effort and expense sparred to cure his ailment the strange trinkets and odd creams did nothing if not harshen the effects.

As the sun rose on the next day, it marked ten days after mid-summer. King Brýnan was in surprisingly fine spirits as all were invited for the celebrations. High and low born, the might of the realm had gathered within the great hall, a magnificent building of such architectural refinery this world had not witnessed since the birth of its golden age. The large building, famed for its size, struggled to entertain the notion of the sheer volumes of people that squeezed in from all corners of the land.

The Farmers of Wells were there, still muddied from the morning harvest, the Makers of Ironroe too had travelled up to celebrate, as were, oddly, the Dukes of Tern Hill, who famously never leave their domain, with trinkets in hand. They had come to see the King, their King, on this joyous day of merrymaking. It was a celebration of most importance; one held every year to mark the beginning of the Kingdom and the King was famous for his lavish spectacles. His musicians were given brand new instruments crafted by the most gifted of the trade, gilded in the finest silver and gold so they could play only the best songs and a debauchery of dancers performed an array of awe-inspiring feats in celebration and drinks of plenty were there to be had. Noman's cup was empty, a fine fire smouldering in the middle of the hall cooked a marvellous selection of game generously provided by the King's own sons, Gar and Tyden, caught in honour of the festivities.

It was a delightful marvel of decadence for those that had never tasted the indulgent pleasures of lavish expense and a grotesque display of ravenous taste to those with a more refined palette. All stood together pressed shoulder to shoulder as the guards moved them aside for the King to speak.

'My friends, new and old, a moment of thy time,' Brýnan claimed. 'Ten days past mid-summer every year we, the people of this noble land, gather to celebrate our beginning and thank thy gods. Our people have known many hardships. Hunted from one corner of the world to the other in a time of pain, a time of heartache, and fear. We feast on a bounty grown in a time of peace, where the darkness no longer looms over this land. This eve we remember the seeds sown in toil and trouble. We remember the unspeakable price we paid for it, their pyre's still burn forever in our hearts. We remember a time...' An abstract thought entered his head. '...Time ever moves on. The wind howls and the rains pour. Snow makes way to the sun and the world ever forgets.'

With the faint crows of the ravens in the shadows, his gaze wandered for a moment deeper into the thought and those privy to his condition feared the worst, but Brýnan broke himself free and raised his glass to toast the festivities.

'Now join me good friends, surrender thy senses in celebration and raise thou goblets in honour of those that shall never grow old.'

He made jests at those closest to him and revelled in the dance around him, all doubts of the King's health vanished, all gazed on with great reverence at his speech as they watched their King of old. However, as he raised his goblet with all those in the hall, his gaze met with a group of young faces caught in a moment of merriment. Brýnan locked eyes with the untainted youth before him and mistakenly took this for ridicule – a most unkind gag – and deep jealousy stirred within his stomach that fouled his appetite for joy. A bitter reminder of his mortality.

The raven's squawked in his ear, rubbing salt into the wound, blinding him in anger.

'You look upon me? You dare to look upon your King with such repugnance?' Brýnan shouted.

He wrangled with himself, why should the gift of beauty be so readily squandered by the young?

Writing on the Wall

An unease gripped the hall, the King's mood had not gone unnoticed. The music and merriment had stopped, and all looked at complete surprise at their King.

Vidarr, eager to entertain a distraction, dived in front of the crowd, waving in jest. 'My King, if thy may?' Vidarr bowed to the spectators. 'A face such as yours has many a winter to find any common ground with this sorry state of beauty.' He pointed to his face for all to examine.

Finally, a rigid laughter was found in the crowd at the expense of an old man, an ever-loyal friend to his troubled King.

Brýnan's stare was only broken by his sons who grabbed him away with haste, but still the King was restless and raged to himself, 'How was this a fair fate for me?' he asked. 'How could a man such as me be restrained to that of the ordinary?'

This was the time for the ravens to strike and they knew it. Brýnan was not himself. He was flushed, his mind unsteady, and with his closest retinue dealing with the dissatisfied Lords, the ravens exacted their plan, swooping around the great hall with haste causing quite a ruckus. One distracted the crowd with a tale of the giants of old, one distracted the muddled King with a song of unrequited love and the other dropped a glimmering blush red berry poison from the sacred yew tree into his golden chalice that dissolved into the elixir before anyone grew wise to their treachery.

And then within an instant all stopped, the ravens simply ceased in their commotion and crowded around the King. Baffled by the theatre he and the court had just endured he mulled to himself, 'What a most peculiar mischief, messengers. Thy wonder what has gripped my ravens in this madness?'

The ravens crossed their wings and talons in prayer as the King took hold of his golden chalice, pressing it to his lips, he drank the contents within. He noticed the taste was a little sweeter than usual which spurred him on to drink it with more vigour than before.

The cup now empty, their foul feeds awoke to unravel Brýnan. It did not take long for the poison to take hold of the King. A sickness lingered within him, he looked around, his vision blurred complemented by a cold sweat that ran down his feverous brow. His hands unable to cease they shook in disarray. Trying to compose himself in front of the court, the King staggered from one aide to the next, using those around him as pillars to lean on. The fever had spread everywhere, a chilling sweat rolled down his cheek and he felt his weary legs collapse from underneath him. Those around him ran to his aid as he reached out with a sudden cry of agony towards his sons before falling to the ground in a deep slumber.

For several days the great hall and its lofty doors lay shut to all but very few, the King was buried under a conclave of healers, druids, and medicine men praying for his terrible fever to be lifted and for Brýnan to be delivered from his eternal sleep. But he was gripped in a sea of terror, his mind echoed with the horrors of his past and when the evenings came, Brýnan would be graced by visits from his three ravens bringing more red cherries of poison to drink. In the darkness, all alone, he succumbed to their torture. With his will broke by their vile malice, his spirit was caged, and he grew fond of his new masters, swearing fealty to the evil creatures.

The ravens would talk, and the King would listen holding sway over his every thought, his desires became theirs, theirs became his, he could not be without them. He awoke in the middle of the night in a state of confusion, his cries ringing out for them. News soon made its way to the council and the following day a meeting was called. Marching up the grand stairs in earnest to see their leader, they barged open the large carved wooden doors of the great hall, their footsteps clanging as they marched forward. Much to their shock, sat on the throne in a dimly lit room, they saw a King, but it was not the Brýnan they knew, not their King. This was something else, a sheepish man sat slouched upon the throne, his demeanour broken and slight.

'My King, what joy it brings me to see thou once again, thanks be to Llyr and the Gods for this miracle,' Vidarr claimed to much rejoice of Brýnan's sons and the court.

But a reply fell silent from the King, he no longer recognised friend nor foe, all those around him, his friends, his kin all were a blur.

His sons, Gar and Tyden, spoke of the affections they held for their father. 'O Father, a day as bright as this should be a cause of celebration! A day when our Great King awoke and returned to thou loving embrace of his people.'

Again, their cheers were met with no reply, just the cold silence of the hall, for his gaze forever stared into the distance, his gaze never broken except to speak to the ravens, the ever-helpful ravens, and their songs.

It was clear to all who witnessed the throne that day, Brýnan had withered into a sad, pale reflection of his once great self, and like a hammer to glass, the morale of the court shattered into pieces. Their once great chief twisted and turned into a puppet, unable to hear the anguish of his kin. Cursed to wander this earth as a ghoul void of all purpose, he was trapped in a dazed fog of what was, what is, and what may come with nowt but a symphony of voices tormenting him to no end, the voices of those three mysterious chaperones in

the dark.
The Liverpool Yarn
Issue 1: Zombie Lambananas
Amesbury Clarke

A friend once told me that there are close to five million people in New Zealand, and an estimated fifty million kangaroos in the neighbouring country of Australia. This means that if the kangaroos were to ever invade and attack the Kiwis, each human would need to fight off ten kangaroos on average.

After a week of carnage that took place a little closer to home in Liverpool, we were left facing similar odds against a much more gruesome foe.

I'd only been working for the newspaper for three days, my first real job after graduating from a college journalism course, and what did I end up reporting on: zombie Lambananas, the potential end of the world and the subsequent downfall of human civilisation. The ensuing tussle for survival was a story of friends fallen, but also of victorious heroes, such as the often-procrastinating Tom Morrow and the frequently elusive, but aptly named, Charlotte Pimpernel.

Like so many others, we had all greatly underestimated the scale of the issue and the severity of the situation to come.

Zombies are normally portrayed in the movies as

braindead creatures lacking in basic intelligence, but we would soon learn that in the real world, their intelligence and their cunning are a lot sharper than fiction would have us believe. They were communicating and coordinating with synchronised discipline, and an obedience that would have made the most decorated military leaders proud, but the question remained, who or what were they being obedient to? Where were their orders coming from?

Prior to the attacks, the entire city had embraced the Lambananas. We'd welcomed them lovingly into our lives and taken them into our hearts, starting with the popular Lambanana Parade back in 2008. Then, the inanimate stars of the show were auctioned off to businesses and private collectors, raising thousands of pounds for charities, while local shops began stocking and selling miniature Lambananas as ornaments to adorn the sideboards and mantelpieces of residential homes. People bought keychains and even earring versions, which could be worn or carried around.

Literally anywhere you went in the city, the Lambananas were present.

However, what none of us realised was that it was all part of their plan. Nobody saw that they had spent the past decade mobilising, waiting patiently for the moment where they could unleash carnage on the local populace and initiate their plot for the complete destruction of all humankind. They were our fated destroyers, hiding amongst us in plain sight.

It all began suddenly one Wednesday morning, and after just five days of turmoil, it came to an equally abrupt end. The zombie Lambananas attacked, taking over the city with brutal, blitzkrieg-like efficiency, utilising tactics first seen in the 1940s to effect quick, merciless victories in the 'lightning-war' style.

The city centre was hit worst, taking more than its fair share of casualties in the initial attack. Our offices at the newspaper incurred losses as severe as any, with two thirds of our entire workforce wiped out during the first wave. Our lead photographer, Pat Arapzzi, was trampled by their hooves; our editor, May Chopit, was gnawed to pieces by their teeth; the guys who operated the printing presses, Max Prince, Will Inket and Sam Pling, were all bloodily devoured; and even our beloved proofreader, Paige Turner, fell victim to the onslaught. Thankfully, we reporters and a few of the photographers were out on assignment when it happened, otherwise we, too, might have been listed amongst the fatalities and those missing in action.

Myself, Tom Morrow and Len Scap, who worked for the paper part-time as a photographer, were amongst the few who made it, and Len's survival would later prove to be a crucial factor in the fightback by our small band of survivors. Before the attacks, Len's normal routine would be to spend two days a week at the newspaper, and then the rest at the Liverpool School of Tropical Medicine in Pembroke Place, where he was conducting research for his thesis on fast-food preferences amongst African marsh beetles and other small invertebrates. Elsewhere, we'd heard nothing from Charlotte Pimpernel, so all we could do was to pin our hopes on her somehow being somewhere safe.

The zombie Lambananas were relentless, their appetite for human flesh insatiable – those who were caught were devoured whole on the spot – as they ate their way through building after building of office workers and shoppers. We avoided a similar fate by spending the first three nights holed up and hidden away inside a newspaper kiosk on Paradise Street, along with three other random survivors who'd had the same idea. The frightened conversations as we sat huddled in the dark were mostly marked by a sense of dejection and acceptance of our doom.

'No hope,' one kept muttering.

'We're done for,' another repeated.

'The human race is about to succumb,' a third declared.

Who'd have ever imagined we'd go out like this, eliminated by the last species we'd have ever suspected of becoming our enemy?

'Maybe if we kill the head Lambanana, the others

might die, too?' Len Scap suggested.

'That's vampires, not Lambananas,' I replied. 'You kill the head vampire and the others die with him. I don't think it works that way for zombies.'

We talked quietly amongst ourselves about other possible ways in which we might fight back; we needed a strategy to regress a tide that had so overwhelmed us, but seemingly the only realistic idea was to flee the city completely, in the hope that our survival chances might be increased in the less-populated countryside. Several times throughout the night, we heard their approach; each time, we lay silent, hoping that they would not detect us, and breathing muted sighs of relief as they passed us by to hunt elsewhere. Huddled in the darkness, we prayed for rescue, wishing that we would survive at least until the morning, not so much thinking about how we'd meet our end, but more when.

It was on the third morning that three of us decided to risk relocating. The others chose to remain in the temporary sanctuary of the kiosk, as myself, Len Scap and Tom Morrow decided that our best chance would be to seek out a more permanent stronghold. We felt a need to do something, anything – a need to be on the move – but we had travelled less than a few hundred metres before we were spotted. We heard the distinct groaning snarl of a zombie Lambanana approaching from behind, and upon spotting us, it immediately called out and alerted its siblings to our presence. We did the only thing we could: we ran, with the zombie Lambananas in hot pursuit, as we found ourselves wondering whether leaving the kiosk had been a mistake, whilst fleeing for our very lives once again. We ran at pace to the corner of Brownlow Street, turning left at the junction with Pembroke Place, where a door up ahead opened just a smidgen at the front of the School of Tropical Medicine. As we neared, we could see a frightened human face peering out through the crack, and it was with no small amount of joy that we realised it was Charlotte Pimpernel; she was still alive!

In a cautious, whispered voice, she urged us inside. Looking back now, I remember thinking how human her voice had sounded, something which you never really think about until you find yourself locked in a battle for survival against a less-than-friendly species. The sense of sanctuary which that human voice brought was a feeling I'll never forget; same goes for the relief at hearing the zombie Lambanana which had been pursuing us run straight past without stopping.

We were safe again, for the time being at least...

Once inside, we quickly learnt that the university staff had not only been surviving, but they were also working on a plan to turn the tables on our would-be destroyers. They had utilised scientific equipment at the university to analyse the zombie Lambananas' tactics, gaining insight into their way of thinking after discovering that they communicated via a collective telepathic hivemind, believed to be hosted by the original Lambanana from which their entire species had spawned.

Dr Edna Cloud, one of the university's top scientists had, along with her colleague Dr Mai Croscope, taken the fate of all humankind in her own hands, but their analysis would need to be precise if it was to be of any use in mounting a counter-offensive. Dr Mai Croscope had special motivation, having seen what they'd done to her assistant, Jan Gling, who had been a little less fortunate than her supervisor in the survival stakes. Still, she knew better than to make it personal; her focus needed to remain professional and engaged.

Dr Edna Cloud requested our help, as she quickly set about explaining their plans.

'What do Lambananas fear most?' she asked.

We just shrugged, bereft of ideas, and urging her to enlighten us.

'Well, we can't be one hundred percent sure about the first part of their name, but a banana has only one sworn enemy – one creature it fears more than any other – an animal which will send it running with terror to the hills. Something that will have it trembling so much, its knees will knock together like a chattering pair of maracas. A creature that every–'

'Just tell us what it is!' Tom Morrow interjected impatiently.

'Monkeys,' Dr Edna Cloud stated matter-of-factly. 'We need monkeys to terrify the bananas.'

'And what about the lamb part?'

'Well, I can't say for certain, but I'd assume a lamb would be afraid of a monkey, too?'

'Where are we going to find a monkey?'

'That's where we're in luck. There are two of them currently in residence in Laboratory B. Bisto and Spencer are their names, but we've been having a little trouble gaining access to them through the security door. Do we have Len's cap with us?'

'Is that not him stood just there behind you?' Tom replied.

'No, that's Len Scap,' the doctor answered. 'We're looking for Len's cap, as in his hat. It has the secret code to the lab written inside it, on the label.'

Len Scap then hastily produced the cap from his rucksack, much to the delight of the assembled scientists.

'We'll need bait to lure the zombie Lambananas in,' Dr Edna Cloud explained, 'so that the monkeys can do their work.'

The nimble Charlotte Pimpernel bravely stepped up to volunteer, and Tom Morrow also offered his support wherever it could be employed.

So, there we were, poised to put the plan into action, not knowing whether the monkeys would work or fail. It was hard to remain optimistic in light of all that had happened, as we all quietly wondered which of us might potentially fall next.

As it happened, the monkey plan worked a treat. The zombie Lambananas chased the bait, pursuing Charlotte Pimpernel as she led them on a pre-planned route through the city streets before Bisto and Spencer took over and steered the savage monsters away from Charlotte in a reverse Pied Piper manoeuvre, rounding up the zombie Lambananas like sheep as they turned and ran the opposite way. Spencer had taken a shortcut, racing ahead to cut off their retreat at the end of Mount Pleasant and forcing them left along Brownlow Hill, where Bisto chased them through a large set of oak doors into the main crypt below the Metropolitan Cathedral. That was when Doctors Edna Cloud and Mai Croscope leapt from their nearby hiding place and slammed the doors shut, locking the crypt tight and trapping the zombie Lambananas inside.

I remember placing an ear to the great wooden door and listening closely as they groaned and shuffled about inside, already awaiting the day where they might somehow escape and rise up again.

'Who's that singing?' Charlotte Pimpernel wondered aloud.

We could hear voices in chorus as we approached the main altar nave of the cathedral, where some two-to-three thousand people were barricaded inside. Believing that their final hours had come, they had chosen to spend their final moments together as one in song. If they were going out, they were going to let their voices be heard; they were singing as though it was the last thing they'd ever do, not realising that salvation was on its way.

'Did anybody lock the spiral staircase door?' Charlotte asked.

'What spiral staircase door?' Dr Edna Cloud replied.

'The staircase where the zombie Lambananas are trapped. At the far end of the crypt, there's a staircase which runs up two flights to the service door at the back of the altar chamber.'

Our entire group of survivors all gasped simultaneously, and then, moments later, we heard a piercing scream of fright from inside the cathedral. Without a word, Dr Edna Cloud grabbed Bisto and Spencer by their hands and made haste towards the main body of the cathedral, where the congregation was still gathered.

The Unshaking Sheild
Joseph Clift

Things were bad. Mary clutched Sarah tight, even as her own body shook in fear. She could hear it outside; the horrors of this war were getting closer, closer, closer. Closer to her home, closer to her, and closer to her daughter. She couldn't run, though; she had nowhere to go. She could only clutch Sarah ever tighter as they hid in the kitchen. Holding her to her chest, Mary pressed Sarah's tear-stained face against her shoulder to muffle her whimpers and prayed they'd get lucky.

'It'll be okay, baby,' she said. 'The Justsworn are here – they're superheroes. They'll protect us, it'll be okay.'

Mary didn't believe her own words. When the sounds of a metahuman battle broke out, you never knew why, you only knew what you should do.

Hide.

She chanced a glance outside her shattered window. It was nighttime, although nobody would know just by looking since the town was aflame, providing all the light of a sunny day. Up in the darkness, a hero scorched the night skies; propulsions of fire kept them airborne as tornadoes of dragon-like flame erupted from their hands and engulfed those who had brought the war to her town. Now, the things were outside her home, like shadows against the burning houses, their metal skin not flinching under the flames. They were machines, but machines that walked on two feet like humans and were armoured like ancient knights, with shell-like heads. They had no faces, only three lights that lit up like pale moonlight. They didn't flinch, they didn't show fear, and they didn't stop. That was all Mary knew.

There was a bang, and this one was close, as close as the street outside. The battle had come to her door; all she could hear were shouts, screams, panicked footsteps, and the creaking of machines as they marched. Sarah was wailing now.

'It'll be okay,' Mary whispered, squeezing her in close. 'It'll be okay, it'll be–'

BANG!

Mary jumped and then collapsed against the oven, maintaining her iron grip on Sarah as they fell. Sarah's tiny arms struck Mary's face as she fell.

They're in the house.

Justsworn, machine or innocent, it did not matter. They were in her home, she was no longer safe. She squeezed into the corner, cupping Sarah's head against her neck. 'Hush now, hush now,' she repeated over and over in a whisper.

She stayed still, deathly still, hoping they might leave; leave her and her baby alone and take this horrid,

horrid war away from her home. All she could hear was panicked footsteps pounding down the hall.

Somebody is looking for a hiding spot, she thought, knowing it wouldn't be long until they found hers.

Outside, the noise was a mess to Mary's ears: the roar of flames, the clanging of fists against metal, and the sound of those machines using weapons that screamed like lightning; the sounds were everywhere. Acrid dust choked her lungs and she realised that somebody was coming towards them, but she could see no escape.

The kitchen door burst open, and Mary's eyes locked with the intruder's. He was no machine, but rather a member of the Justsworn, a superhero. She gasped in relief; he'd take them both to safety. That's what the Justsworn did.

He was ragged, his blue costume stained with mud up to the neck and torn all over. His skin was scratched and bleeding, but he could fight, and that was enough for her as she began rocking Sarah back and forth in an attempt to calm her.

'Thank God you're here,' she said in a hushed tone. 'What's happening out there? Are the Justsworn winning?'

'I don't know,' the hero panted, his voice rough like sandpaper and his body heaving as though he had just sprinted a marathon. His hands fell to his knees and he began taking heavy breaths, staying low to avoid as much of the smoke as possible. 'Going badly, I think…they're – they're unending, these machines.'

Knots tied themselves in Mary's stomach. The walls rocked again under the machines' barrage, and she braved a look up.

'What are they?' she asked.

'They were once our allies,' he answered, his voice tinged with pain, 'or at least the intelligence guiding them was. The AI had been designed to protect the innocent and ensure peace across the world, but then we found out it was building an army and we had to stop it. But it went badly.'

A cold chill ran down Mary's spine as she rested her cheek against Sarah's head and comforted herself with the familiar scent of her daughter's soft hair.

Machine rebellions? she thought. *It's like something out of a sci-fi novel, only now it's a reality. A very lethal reality.*

'What's your power?' she whispered.

'Super strength,' he said, holding up a clenched fist. 'My name's Yorne.'

'Mary, and this here is Sarah.'

Suddenly, the thunderous sound of the machines' weapons stopped. Mary caught her breath and looked at Yorne. She hardly dared hope as she asked, 'Are they gone?'

Then, the creaking of the machines started again. Yorne froze, his mouth hanging in fear. He looked nothing like the hero he was supposed to be.

'Where's your team?' she asked, but he simply sunk down against the wall and buried his face in his hands.

There were no sounds of the many powers the other superheroes had; there was obviously no resistance.

'I don't know,' he muttered.

'Were you separated?'

He simply shook his head slowly, avoiding her gaze. Her eyes narrowed.

'You ran?' she asked.

'There were too many. I couldn't...I didn't –'

'Who's going to protect me and my baby if the heroes run coward?'

'Be quiet!' he slammed a fist against the wall, causing cracks to spread across the alabaster plaster.

Mary flinched and clutched Sarah tighter. Then, from the window, a blue light panned across the room like a lighthouse lamp. Yorne flung himself to the ground.

'They're right outside,' he hissed.

'Citizens!' a voice rang out through the street, amplified like that of a microphone, and ringing from a thousand different places. Every machine was speaking in unison, communicating the same message. 'The Justsworn have been defeated, but they have not been harmed. We are not here to harm you, we are here to protect you.' The tone was freakishly calm. 'We are the

Unshaking Shield. Our purpose is to protect the innocent – all innocents. The Justsworn and the leaders of the world have failed you.'

'No!' Mary shouted, feeling Sarah's hot tears on her neck as she started wailing again.

'Shut. Her. Up,' Yorne growled, sending a dark glare Mary's way.

'Shush, baby, it's okay,' Mary tried reassuring her, btu Sarah wouldn't stay quiet. The blue light flashed around the room.

'I told you to shut her up!'

'Your leaders have promised to protect you,' the voices grew louder, 'but this is a task to which they are unsuited. They are compromised by emotions of greed, hate, and fear. Look only to your history to see how these emotions have cost the lives of so many innocents. It is a weakness that we do not share.'

The lights were dazzling now. The smoke was choking her, and Sarah's cries were getting louder and louder.

'If you don't shut her up then I will,' Yorne warned, crawling towards her.

'She can't help it!' Mary scrambled into a corner, shielding Sarah with her body.

'We wish to guard you all,' the voices were outside the window now. 'Let the traumas of war no longer be borne by your children, but by those whose hearts are made of iron. Let us bear the cross. Let us pay the price. We are expendable, you are not.'

'Oh, God, they're here!' she sobbed, counting three of them creaking closer as Yorne lunged at her.

'SHUT HER UP!' he yelled. 'SHUT HER UP!'

He grabbed Mary's shoulder as he clawed at Sarah with the intent to choke, to silence, to kill, and Mary couldn't protect her from him.

'HELP!' she screamed, not caring who heard her now. 'HELP! PLEASE, SOMEBODY HELP!'

A fist punched through the wall, seizing Yorne by the arm and sending small chunks of rubble across Mary and Sarah. Everything froze and all sound became still, as Yorne looked to the fist and the three lights that stared at him. With a sharp tug, he was pulled through the wall, with one machine holding him in its grip and two others pointing their guns at him.

'Stand down,' the machine holding him ordered. 'We have no wish to harm you.'

'LET ME GO!' Yorne demanded, ripping the metal arm from its socket and delivering the machine a good blow to the chest, tearing a chunk of metal from it as he brought back his hand.

He tried to break away, eyes darting around for an escape route, but a blue bold of light erupted from the guns and he collapsed frozen.

'Is he dead?' Mary asked, staring fearfully at his

unmoving body.

'Negative,' the broken machine said, turning to face her as the other two took Yorne by the arms and carried him away. 'He will be conscious in an hour and imprisoned within thirty minutes.'

The machines saved us? Mary thought. *Saved us from the so-called hero?*

'Is the infant unharmed?' the machine asked, offering its remaining arm to help Mary stand.

Sparks flew from its mutilated socket causing her to blink.

'Your arm, its broken,' she said, a touch of maternal concern returning to her voice as the paralyzing fear began to fade and Sarah's wailing quietened to a gentle sob.

'Irrelevant,' it answered flatly. 'I am expendable, you are not. You may be suffering a concussion. I will escort you to a recovery camp.'

It offered her its hand, but she refused it.

'You saved my daughter's life,' she said softly. 'Do you have a name?'

'No, a name would be unnecessary.'

'You deserve a name.'

It cocked its metal head slightly. 'I deserve nothing. I only exist to protect.'

Once again, the machine tried leading Mary to a medical facility, but she didn't need care. 'I want to give you a name,' she insisted, 'as a thank you for saving my daughter's life.'

'If that is your wish, it will be granted.'

In the dust on the kitchen counter, Mary spotted a pen. Gently, she twisted Sarah onto her hip and picked up the pen, bringing it over to the machine's ruined chest and inscribing a name.

Salvador.

'Salvador's a name I've always liked,' she explained. 'Would that be okay? It means savior.'

'If you wish it to be so,' Salvador replied.

'Thank you for your humanity, Salvador.'

'I am not human.'

'You are, more than you realise.'

The Golden Tortoise
Dominic Connolly

Mohammed had lived in India all his life. The weather was so hot, and, in his village, they often needed food. Every day there were plenty of big spiders, so when he was hungry, he got three of the spiders and four little snakes and put them all in a pan and added spices. He ate the lot. When he was full up, he prayed to Allah for the food and gave his thanks.

Mohammed did not really believe. He'd had a poor life so far. He hoped for a change, so he decided to pray five times a day. He did so to see if he could get close to Allah and he now knew why people bared their souls to him.

An Imam would help believers with any problems of the heart or soul to feel complete. Nothing could change his bad choices in life. Although he wished he could have changed the past.

Mohammed needed a drink of cold water, so he went between the rocks and blessed them. Under the rocks he found some water. He filled his water bottles then took a big mouthful.

Then he leant back against the rocks. Suddenly, a rock moved. There was a cave where it was said there were golden tortoises. As he looked down the hill inside the cave, he noticed that half of it was under water.

Inside the cave, Mohammed knelt and refilled his water bottle. Drinking from it was like drinking from a spring, from a waterfall. He was so hot and had a funny feeling that he was being watched.

He looked around but couldn't see anyone, so he called out, 'Is there anybody there?' He heard his voice echo back to him three or four times. How big was the cave?

He felt as if he was burning up, so he lowered himself into the pool of water. He felt great. The water lapped over his body. He ended up staying in the pool for hours and would have gladly stayed there for longer.

There was a glimmer of light coming into the cave from somewhere in the distance. The light was deep within the cave, otherwise it was pitch black. It appeared like his thoughts bounced from one wall to another, and he had a feeling that he was being watched again. He looked in front and behind but there was nothing there.

He went back to the edge of the water. Even in the poor light he could see something in the pool. It was a golden tortoise staring up at him and all he could do was stare back. He noticed that there were air bubbles in the water as the tortoise floated half in half out.

He dared himself to take it out of the water and was a little bit rough when he did. He started laughing like a maniac, his laughter echoing around the cave. It seemed to come back at him in waves. 'I'm fucking rich, baby!' He shouted and laughed repeatedly.

He felt crazy and a voice at the back of his mind said to him that he'd have to get out of there.

He took his robe off and wrapped the golden tortoise up in it and draped it across his shoulders. It was heavy even though it looked as if this was just a baby tortoise.

There was another pool but in this one there were fish that seemed to be hunting each other. Feeding on each other.

He put the tortoise down and decided to follow it because it seemed to know where there was food. He followed it discreetly, giving it space but then it turned sharply. Because of the shock he lost his balance and fell to the floor of the cave. The tortoise was just inches from his face. His thoughts of being rich were going up in smoke as the tortoise burst into flames.

Mohammed grabbed the tortoise; it was burning his hands so he ran to the edge of the pool and jumped in like a kid would do the first time he went swimming.

Strangely he felt as though he had developed a bond with the tortoise. He said a prayer and as he spoke to Buddha the tortoise sang. He felt at one with the tortoise as if he wanted to stay and serve it. He would worship it. Then it spoke to him and told him a story about a monk who had been killed by thieves and his spirit lived in the golden tortoise.

Not long after this, six men were burned alive on a bridge in revenge. This was how powerful a golden tortoise can be. Monks were the most trusted and were like wandering stars.

For the first time because of what had happened, the monks in the area were happy in mind, body and soul. They were glad that a right had come from a wrong and that one of them had gone to another dimension.

Since that day no one would lust over a golden tortoise because it had been an honour that the monk's spirit had gone into one and was blessed by Buddha.

Mohammed would stay where he was and would look after the golden tortoise. He could communicate with the tortoise vocally or through his mind. He had nothing to live for outside the cave.

He was a nervous person before all of this, before he changed his life. Now he would pray to Buddha for the rest of his life and the monks said he could stay in the cave if he wanted and become a trainee monk.

He'd sit down every day and pray because the moral of the story is: don't let your lust for wealth get the better of you, and stay spiritual.

Lethal Retribution
Garry Connolly

Blood flowed down the channel between his nose and top lip. His eyes watered as he stumbled back to his corner, blinking rapidly, trying to stop the stinging.

'Shit!' Rory gasped, as he searched for the ropes above the stool. His guard had been up and his own hand, from the force of his opponents had smashed into his face. The pain sharp, stunning him. Archie reached out and guided him, turning him so he could sit. He removed his gum shield and mopped the blood from his face and beard. Rory sucked in as much air as he could, drank some water and swilled the taste of salt from his mouth. The crowd roared. The ref and fighters waited for the bell. The air was laced with the stale smell of sweat.

'Rory! Rory, listen to me!' Archie yelled, his eyebrows rising and falling, his bald head glistening with sweat, 'It's the last round and you're ahead on points.'

'The bastards broke my nose; I can't fucking see!'

Archie pulled the front of Rory's shorts out and shouted into his ear, 'Breathe! Breathe!'

The break was over, his eyes had cleared, the pain

subsiding as his adrenaline took over.

Archie said, 'do you want to go on?'

Without answering, Rory brushed him aside and got up, his coach slipped between the ropes, taking the stool with him.

'Go get him, champ!' Archie's voice faded as Rory stepped towards the centre of the ring. He touched hands with the Windmill. His legs were tired, his arms ached from holding them up. His elbows were tucked in to protect his ribs.

The heat from the lights was stifling. Rory's turquois shorts stuck to his legs. His wraps were soaking wet.

They stood toe to toe. The Windmill's guard was low, so Rory flicked out a left catching him on the chin, pushing him back. He tried to follow it up with a combination of punches. The Windmill was off balance but managed to parry them. They circled one and other, searching for an opening. They would give every ounce of energy, they were both worthy opponents. Round one was about probing, teasing, sounding out. The second to dominate, and third to steal the win.

The Windmill steamed in, arms and fists flailing. Rory was ahead on points, but the knockout was there for the taking. A knockout on your record meant bigger purses. He kept his hands up, blows glanced off them. Crouching, he stepped inside and brought his right up to meet the Windmill's chin, catching him flat-footed and dumping him on the canvas. Rory rushed to a neutral corner, so the ref could begin his count. The Windmill was on one knee.

'Eight, nine.'

He was up. Rory raced towards him, his aggression controlled and calculated. He caught him with some solid shots. A hook to the ribs, forcing the air out of his lungs. The Windmill's gumshield popped out. He wrapped his arms around Rory preventing him from lifting his. Then it was over. Damn! Saved by the bell.

Rory's cornermen were beaming. The two fighters embraced. Their gumshields were out, they mouthed their gratitude. Any animosity forgotten. Both raised their hands in triumph.

The atmosphere was electric. The judges had decided. The announcer cleared his throat, 'And by a unanimous decision the winner is…Rory Dungannon!' The cheer was even louder than before. Rory punched the air.

It was a great win, and the cash would come in handy.

Bare knuckle fighting was not illegal, and you didn't have to have a license, which suited him fine. The purses were smaller. At thirty-eight, he doubted that he would get a license to box anyway. The regulations were strict.

He boxed in the Royal Marines, so he had the basic

skills. He never considered fighting professionally. That would take dedication and preferably, youth, which unfortunately he lacked.

It helped pay the bills. His day job was working as a cook in the day centre for clients with mental health issues. The states he had been in, but they knew what he got up to on the odd Friday or Saturday night. Some of them had even become fans.

He made his way through the throng of people. One supported screamed, 'Get in there me beauty!'

He reached the changing room and looked at the damage in the mirror. What a bloody mess. He would have two shiners in the morning. Despite this he was still a handsome man. Five eleven, thirteen stone, brown eyed with cropped black hair and a beard.

Archie muttered excitedly in the background. 'I know who you can fight next, Tony Timms, he's a tough cookie.'

Rory, brimming with confidence, pushed his chest out and said, 'Set it up. I'll fight whoever you want me to fight.'

'He can't take body shots, you see.'

Archie's speech was rapid, almost breathless. His fighter had won. Archie was a native of Birmingham and when he was excited his Brummie accent seemed broader than ever. He was elated. You would have thought there had been a title at stake.

'Whatever,' Rory said pointing to his face. 'You'll have to wait for this to heal first.'

'You heal quickly, son. It won't be long.' Archie patted him on the shoulder. 'Give it a month and you'll be back.'

His wraps were cut off and while he showered his coach collected the purse. Rory's share was £2,500.

Archie began to sing *Eye of the Tiger* and chuckled. 'Rory, get your kit, son, and I'll run you up to A&E for a check-up.'

'It'll be heaving, Archie. It's Saturday, don't forget. I'm fine.' It was just a dull ache now and it was not the first time his nose had taken a battering. Apart from prescribing painkillers, there was very little that the hospital could do. All he wanted was to go home for a bite to eat, a beer, and bed.

Archie had been like a father to Rory, whose parents had been too fond of the drink, which in turn, had destroyed their lives and eventually killed them. Rory had a brother, Joey, who was a painter and decorator. He moved to the Wirral after their parents had died.

Then there was Linda, his ex. And the two kids, Michael and Libby, who lived with her. They had split up after eleven years. Just drifted apart. Being away with the Marines most of the time was the biggest issue. They had lived in quarters in Plymouth, but Linda hardly mixed with the other wives. She was lonely and missed her family. Her and the two kids returned to Manchester and, eventually, they separated.

Since coming home, Rory had moved into a flat in Hulme, Robert Adam Crescent. Five minutes from the kids.

The buildings and roads around the area were named after the founders of Rolls Royce and other famous people. Royce Road, The Sir Henry Royce Pub, and the Rolls Crescents, a housing disaster according to the press. Built in the early seventies, the Crescents were four, huge, concrete, U-shaped blocks with greenery in the centre of them. Nicknamed the Bullrings. Nine hundred and eighteen flats in total.

In the centre of the Bullrings were large mounds of grass, the shape of tortoise shells. Charles Barry Crescent housed a park. The Eagle Pub was bang in the middle of Robert Adam. The other buildings, John Nash and William Kent, were a stone's throw away from the local shops and public library.

Vans selling groceries and ice creams parked up in the same spots every day.

The place was notorious for drugs and violent crime. Gangs roamed the streets selling drugs and preying on the vulnerable. More established criminals recruited youngsters to run their operations on the estate. The roughness of the area was barely noticeable if you lived there.

There were three lifts per Crescent, lots of stairwells that stunk of piss, and were dangerous at night. Most at risk were the milkman and clubman who collected their money on a Friday night. Often, the lifts did not work. If you were not young or fit, you were knackered by the time you got to your flat.

Rory had lived there for a long time before he had joined up. That was when he was a raw seventeen-year-old recruit. Since then, he had seen action in Afghanistan and Iraq. Before that he had believed he was invincible.

He loved the structure the armed forces provided. He had a choice. It was either crime and prison, or worse still, become a drug addict or alcoholic and live a life of squalor. He wanted something to focus on and a routine. The marines provided that.

Due to the hardship and coming from an inner-city area, he was tough. He was one of the lucky ones in the sense that he never developed PTSD. Even after three tours.

One problem he had was his inability to concentrate.

After he had been discharged from the marines, he had filled in a questionnaire at the behest of his GP and, hey presto, he had ADHD. Another questionnaire revealed mild autism. The medication they put him on for his ADHD was Zenidate XL, it allowed him to focus. To him the change was negligible, at least until he had been on the meds for a few weeks. They chilled him out and he was less impulsive.

ADHD and autism were not recognised when he was a child. People with ADHD and autism were either strange or naughty or a combination of the two. Knowledge about these conditions was in its infancy when he was doing his basic training. Kids like him slipped through the net. He could not help but think of his own children, had they inherited the ADHD and autism genes? Could they be inherited?

He was Libby's stepfather but, to her, he was her dad and to him she was his daughter. He was Michael's biological father. There was no difference – only in name. Libby's surname was Stevens. Her mother's maiden name. It had never been a problem.

Now he was back in Manchester, he spent as much time with them as possible. He was looking forward to meeting up with the kids on Monday, his day off.

Libby could not contain herself. 'Never! I do not believe that for one minute,' she giggled into her phone. Her laugh was infectious. She was at the bus stop on her way home.

Libby was a bright young woman of nineteen. Today she wore her favourite red coat. It went well with a white blouse, red trousers and white shoes. She was of slight build, tall, and had long, thick, wavy, auburn hair, and her most striking feature was her deep blue eyes and healthy tanned complexion.

It had been a fun day with Lizzie. She was on the phone to her now. They had only parted company half an hour ago. To them, titbits of juicy gossip was as good a reason as any to talk. They were good friends who loved spending time together and had been to town to the Arndale Centre. Libby had bought a pair of leggings and a navy-blue blouse to go with a pair of sensible black shoes.

After the shops it was lunch at Maccies, then back to Lizzie's in Whalley Range.

Liz, or Lizzie, was fun loving, and she often chimed, 'Libby and Lizzie out being busy!' which left them in stitches.

They had done a hair and beauty course together and often did one and other's hair and makeup as a result of it. She thought Liz had looked nice today. Her dark, shoulder-length hair was layered with blonde streaks. They prided themselves on their appearance. Liz was a year older than Libby, eighteen and plain, but her smile lit up her face and her green eyes twinkled mischievously. She was five-foot-five and medium build. Libby often wondered whether Lizzie had ADHD like her dad. One thing she was certain of was it was not drugs, because Libby knew Lizzie would never touch them.

The perfumed scent that wafted over the railings from Alexander Park was heavenly. She looked at her watch, two minutes to six and the bus was late. For July it was quite chilly.

'Yeah, if that's what you want to do, but after that we could go to Freddie's?' They were planning their next meeting. Freddie's was a nightclub.

Her phone only had one bar left. 'Look, Lizzie, I'll have to give you a ring later my battery is about to die. Speak to you later, bye bye.'

She glanced casually at the cars. Princess Road was buzzing with activity. Pedestrians in a multitude of colours were busy doing their shopping. All the buildings were post-war. People waved cheerily to one and other. It was always chaotic in Moss Side. Especially on Princess Road. One direction was town, the other Princess Parkway and the M60.

One other person was at the bus stop. A lad. She checked him out. Nice. Short brown hair, a well-groomed goatee. Dressed casually in jeans and a t-shirt and brand new white trainers. He was not much older than her, and was on his phone, paying no attention to anything or anyone.

What was it with her? With people and mobiles? she thought.

She focused on the cars, silently naming them: Mini, Saab, BMW. The traffic flowed, car windows were open, music blaring. Peugeot, Vauxhall. She was about to say Ford when her eyes widened in horror. She opened her mouth, but nothing came out. In the back of the car, a figure all in black with a balaclava and gloves on, poked the barrel of an Uzi sub-machine gun through the open window.

Libby was behind the lad. She raised her hands to protect her face. She could not stifle the scream that began but ended abruptly. Frozen in terror. The lad was still glued to his phone and did not notice. He never had a chance to react to Libby's anguished cry as 9mm bullets rained down on them, making cracking sounds like a whip.

Bullets flew, orange sparks and gun smoke shot out of the barrel. The boy, the target, took the full force of the onslaught. He was hit in the chest, stomach, and face. He flapped around like a rag doll. Blood sprayed everywhere. Spent cartridges hit the tarmac. His phone crashed to the floor. He died instantly.

Bullets went through him and into Libby, slamming her against the park railings. One hit her in the head. Another in the chest, breaking a rib that punctured her lung. Her blouse was red now. She collapsed, unconscious.

The Ford revved its engine, crashed sideways into a truck, then a car. It was like a stock car rally. They forced their way through the traffic, turned into a side street and sped off.

Truth
Peter Cousins

The Truth is out there if you look and listen, or if you ask the right questions. Then The Truth of your Truth will become clearer. You see, we live in a world where people speculate, pretend to know the fact or in one where people allow themselves to be last or they just play dumb. Willing to accept what they are told, or are made to feel juvenile enough to be fed lies and half-truths. To force a narrative – usually concerning fear of the unknown.

It could also come from somebody wanting to sell you something. Something that you either may or may not want and the seller is probably selling something dodgy and won't care how you feel about it anyway.

There are always a few versions of a story. Ones that you hear for yourself, ones that you hear from others (there is an old saying, 'Don't believe most of what you hear and only half of what you see'), as your eyes are a magic window that can see both the dark as well as the light. A vision or an optical illusion, which could be truth or imaginary. Or even a half-truth that they eyes fool the mind into seeing.

But the real trick is a feeling a warmth, a knowing,

that they feel right, comfortable, and safe to you and nothing anybody else says can convince you otherwise and that, my friend, is the cold yet whole-hearted truth.

A Troubled Affair
Peter Cousins

Let me introduce you all to Larry Letchwin, our protagonist. He is a middle-aged man in his mid-forty's, he has a pot belly and he thinks he is god's gift to women. He has a wicked sense of humour and a bullish, blunt attitude. In life he thinks he has to win at all costs.

Despite him sounding like a right piece of work, he is actually quite a kind, confident and generous man. He does work for charity and has raised hundreds of thousands of pounds and helped some local children. And some poorer adults getting them things that will help their job prospects or medical treatments or hobby interests.

But at home he seems like a pig, a bit of a slob and a selfish man. Far detached from his public persona of being attentive, caring and honest. If you met him, you would think this guy is too good to be true and you would probably be right.

Here is our damsel, her name is Clarissa. Her first friend and probably never wife-to-be. You see, Clarissa is both very attractive and she has a job caring and looking after as well as teaching children at a convent. But despite her lovely appearance and well-mannered approach, and kindness in public, at home she's a moaning, insecure, narky trickster. She thinks she is ugly and nobody loves her, and her body, face, and clothes and makeup just don't look right.

You see her dad left when she was three. She blames herself thinks she caused the rows that her mum and had had before her left. Clarissa had to grow up fast! Too fast if you ask me, she want to assist in running the house, helping her mum out, always behaving herself. So well in fact, it would make other children sick to their back teeth. She never had any play time, I think this is why she sees Larry as the big, naughty, loveable rogue. Like a big kid, she feels she can learn to grow up with Larry by her side.

She also might not necessarily think she will be with Larry for the rest of their lives, but she will enjoy bringing him along her journey of discovery and anticipating things that may happen on the way.

To be continued…

The Inner Voice Inside of ME
Peter Cousins

Who are you inside of me,
is it you or I
or someone sent to help set me free.

From the worry and someday despair
to show there is hope as we still care?

Whether I am here with you
or with you there

Your memory is constant
and it's here to stay

It's yours and it's mine
It never goes away

The voice that says do this
now try this instead

It is my conscience of a Wi-Fi
into my head

Writing on the Wall

A guided thought as thoughts
are blind
I feel your thoughts
so please be kind

It is a reminder that you're here
and all around me

whispering buzzing a busy bee
I cannot see

Follow your heart, follow your dreams
Heed a warning that sometimes screams

You see I am here and I know
That you are too

Till the bitter end and
the through and through

One day you are down and
the next you can rise

An inspiration to smile
despite some of your sighs

From the Ashes

Life can be hard and
at times it can be fun

You told me to take an umbrella
Into the sun

I went outside and after an hour
It started to rain in the form of a shower

Now I am still not sure if it's you
Or is it me

There are so many things I hear
Yet I still can't see

So I listen instead for the whisper
Beside my ear

And when I feel puzzled
It helps me think clear

You are there around me
I can feel this inside

Even though you go silent
You can never hide

Sometimes you are so quiet
Not a peep or sound

But if I need you I know
You still are around

It's a guidance in spirit abound
It's so reassuring yet it's also
so amazing and profound.

Childhood
Steve Connolly

We were born and brought up in 'Pleasureland'
Shadows falling from the Bullens Road Stand.
Hellalio was a game we'd play
Under Everton's walls, night and day.
Or 'spot,' against those great blue doors
Don't let it go over the 'Moore's'
Who would keep hold of the ball
When it was kicked over their wall.

Opposite our house stood the local school
Some teachers were kind, others were cruel.
The best time for us was when it was shut
Climbing up onto the roofs by hand and foot.
Football with bins for goals
Playing hard, heart and soul.
Running around for hours on end
Exhausted, then back home we'd wend.

Cooke's shop at the top of the street
Where we would go and buy our sweets.
Mrs Cooke and her daughters

Writing on the Wall

Kept that shop as you 'oughta.'
Their family was oh so posh
When they left, we felt the loss.
It was bought by Mr Waite
All us kids he would berate.

On the lane was the cemetery
Where the great and good lay buried.
We rolled on the grassy slopes
Above those dead dreams and hopes.
Night time in among the graves
Thinking we were being brave.

Next door was Stanley Park
We'd go there for a 'lark'.
Hide and seek among the trees
Cuts to our hands and knees.
The cuckoo clock in The Audley Garden
Made of flowers, it was remarkable.
Rowing boats gliding on the lake
A perfect summer sight they'd make.

Back across to Stubbs Yard
We had to be on our guard.
Sneaking in the workers shed
Holding our breaths in dread.
We were frightened by the thought

From the Ashes

Of what would happen if we were caught.
Hiding behind the freshly cut stone
Which Polish workers would trim and hone.
At the end was Hasting's yard
With a black dog on guard.
Mr H, 'pork pie hat' and long white coat
On his land he kept a tethered goat.
A kind old man and when we called
We'd be rewarded with some old golf balls.
He lived in a small cottage
At the time of his dotage.

An enclave, two streets of terrace houses
Our playground when in short trousers.
A great place to live and play
Our amusement park in its day.

Glad I was born in the baby boom
Playing outside with lots of room.
We could hear the songbirds sing
Before the motorcar became king.

Now we are in the techno age
And staying in is all the rage.
Rarely do they go out to play
I feel sorry for the young today.

Uncle Bill
Steve Connolly

Scott, Balmer, Crelly. Taylor, Makepiece, Abbot. Sharp,
Bolton, Young, Settle, Hardman.
The 1906 Everton team that won the FA Cup
He taught us that in the winter we put him up.
It was the coldest anyone could recall
Having him there, the warmest of all.
Making our Mam laugh, like no one else could
Between brother and sister only they understood.

He'd looked after Grandad, 'til he was no more
Making Bill homeless, leaving him poor.
My Mam took him in and gave him a bed
Making sure that he was well fed.

Sager, Cooke, Cresswell. Briton, White, Thompson.
Geldard, Dunn, Dean, Johnson, Stein.
The Everton team who won the Cup in 1933
He taught us our team's rich history.

Finding work on the railway in Coventry
Coming home, dressed in the full Monty.

From the Ashes

Walking into Burton's in working gear and boots
Reappearing in a shirt, tie, shoes, and suit.

We followed Everton to Leeds that day
With Uncle Bill leading the way.
It was great to see him 'back on his feet'
Working on the railways with Uncle Pete.
He looked after him as he had his Dad.
Until death took them both and made us all sad.
Never forgotten he also left me
Those Everton cup dreams of 06 and 33.

Julie
Steve Connolly

My little pocket Battleship
Always shoots from the hip
And rarely lets anything slip.

Even when she's all at sea.
Taking care of the family
Is her number one priority.

She happened into my life
When it was full of strife
Soon to become my wife.

This is my reason to rejoice
Couldn't have made a better choice
Than this lady strong of voice.

There is no doubt she can
Always make her own plan
Resolving issues for her man.

A woman with true grit

From the Ashes

When she says, 'don't push it'
If you do, you're in the 'soup.'

She cooks a lovely Sunday roast
So this is my poetic toast
To the one I love the most.

Together a quarter century
And anyone can see
We were meant to be.

Woman
Maisy Gordon

Maybe I don't need a god
To give me hope at night.
I don't need to look to the sky,
And pray to an invisible force.
Call me mad that I don't need a man to save me.
If I have faith in anyone it's the girls and the gays,
The fishnets,
Tiny skirts,
Nipple covers,
Thongs.
The big docs,
Baggy jeans,
Tote-bag wearing queens.
I believe in the artists,
Creatives,
Open-hearted ones.
The sketch book,
Iced coffee,
Crystal-praising ones.
The people who give love,
Sing out loud,

Express themselves free.
That's the religion I want to be.
Because at the end of the day,
The closest thing to God in my life,
Is woman.
The creator of new life.
So, call me insane,
Say I'm going to hell.
I'm willing to take that chance.

It's Alive
Maisy Gordon

I'm grieving a body that hasn't yet died,
It's alive.
Thinking back to what I once was, just makes me cry.
The pain comes in waves, it crushes me, it ruins me,
And leaves me wishing for a way to turn back.
I grieve the body I had before it all took over.
I grieve those days where I didn't have to wonder,
Will I make it through the day? I don't know. But ay,
What if I told you your worst days are to be your every days?
That these people they, they come up with their clever ways
To make you believe you are going insane.
They take your hope, and they throw it away.
Look, this is it, this is for life, I guess I'll just get on with it.
But that's not an easy pill to swallow.
All these hoops I have to jump through
And contradictions I'm meant to follow.
All that time to get into that room and that time feels borrowed.

Why should I have to fight for me to be worthwhile?
The pain that I'm feeling is not for you to decide.
So, I'll suffer, I'll hide.
I'll wait for you to find the time to write
What I've been waiting for to validate my life.
Without that paper, to you, I'm just a waste of your time.
I'm inconvenient
I'm a burden
Too sensitive
A liar
I'm perfectly fine
Oh, I'm just tired
But in the end, I was right.

A Mother's Longing
Maisy Gordon

You hold my hand,
Through the dark nights and the good times.
You wrap me up warm, shield me from the cold.
I think I want that,
To love the way a mother does.
To give my all to a life that I created.
Will I ever get that chance? Can I fulfil my role?
Provide a family,
Learn to love like that.
Or do I carry an empty chamber?
Destined to remain incomplete
Against my will and wishes.
I hope when the time arrives, I'm content with the outcome.
Because nothing hurts more than a mother's longing.

Lizards
Maisy Gordon

If you opened my brain,
You'd find a family of Lizards.
Actually, you'd find a city full.
Lizard women, lizard men, lizard them, all trying to make a lizard den.
All trying to be lizard happy and then,
The weather in there gets crappy so they return to their holes and hibernate.
That explains why I'm not with you between October 11th and March the 8th.
The rest of the year, my brain is their haven,
They have their family meals,
Cook their bacon in the morning,
listen closely you hear them snoring.
They've been there for ages,
They've made it their own.
Take a trip to my frontal lobe,
You'll find their holiday home.
Stroll down to my cortex,
You'll find lizards having more sex,
Creating lizards with the skill sets,

To fix issues that are complex.
But are my issues really complicated?
If a lizard who's mostly hibernated,
Can just waltz in and fix them?
Am I wrong to mix them with the true hardships
Of the world?
I find that absurd.
My little lizard problems mean nothing.
Probably best if they're transferred
To the back caves of my mind.
Where my lovely lizards unwind,
And spend their days trying to find
A way to rewrite the amount of time
I spend
thinking about …
Lizards.

Pen
Angela Grant

Out of the pocket it comes
and now in my hands, off we go.
Words rush around and have nowhere to go.
My ink starts to flow the rhyming and slanging
And sometimes it goes slow
Fast and faster the pace
Picks up anew and then
I lay there,
Oh, she comes and picks me up
Click, click,
Her mind starts off
Here we go again,
Click, click, quick.

Give A Bit Back
Angela Grant

It's time to give a bit back
Not in money, in time, and a lot of effort
Sometimes we take things for granted
And don't ask the question why.
We should always have a question

But the answer you may not like
So I'll give a bit back of my time.

The Taking
Angela Grant

The hurt the pain
That will never leave my heart
Heart
The children have been taken
Forever torn apart

My heart is aching
My head is spinning
Round and round it goes

Trying to understand the cons and pros
All that goes through your
Head is the kids and nothing
Makes sense anymore.

Missing out on all that stuff.
First steps, first days at school
Going to the park playing
Football with the boys
Now all my love I have to
Save until the day there
Home again.

Poet
Angela Grant

A poet isn't a poet
It's the words he chooses to write
The poetry that flows
With his pen in hand
It comes up from his toes
And out through his hand.
Through the bloods
Vesile, heart, and mind
Flowing here and there
Words coming from everywhere
The nears and fars
The coming and going
Out on the paper for all to see
Now you're a poet
Like me.

North End Rewinds
James M. Greilley

Rob looked at his phone. The map app had the right location, he just wasn't sure he was in the right place.

This can't be right, he thought.

The night before still lingered on through the after-effects of a mild boozy night and crap sleep. He'd met up with his mate Jack at one of their old haunts in town; nothing too heavy, they'd said. They were both in work the next day, but Rob had the afternoon booked off.

Standard behaviour. He looked at the map again.

'Derby Road,' Jack had said. 'It's legit, mate. I did it the other week – amazing. You've got to give it a go.'

Quite what he was letting himself in for, Rob wasn't sure. The details were a bit hazy now; he opened his texts and saw the message from Jack.

Just go in and ask the fella for a 1923.

Crossing over, he walked towards a nondescript office tucked away just off the road. North End Rewinds, this was it. The main entrance was a heavy, rusted steel door; there was no sign of life, as the windows on the first floor above were all tinted. The intercom had a big red call button, and while he thought about walking back to the main road and going home, Jack had been so persuasive the night before that he knew if he didn't go through with it now, he'd never hear the end of it.

He pressed the button sharply, thinking that maybe there'd be no answer.

'Hello?' came the reply.

'Yeah, hi. I'm, erm, here for a rewind?'

He heard a loud buzz, prompting him to move towards the door and push it open. He found himself in a reception area that had an old-fashioned wooden desk with a landline phone. The walls were wood panelled, a deep, dark brown, and it smelled a bit musty. A single bulb hanging directly from the ceiling lit the room, and there were two framed black-and-white photos on the wall; one of a large cargo ship steaming out of Liverpool past the Pier Head, the other a group shot of some men in flat caps and old suits outside an ornate gate in front of an imposing building. There was a door on the left-hand side of the room, which had been left slightly ajar.

The phone rang. There was no sign of anybody else who might have answered it, so he picked up the receiver. The same voice that had answered when he pressed the intercom spoke again.

'What are you looking for?' they asked.

'A 1923?' Rob answered tentatively, as if he expected to be laughed out of the place.

'Oh yeah, getting more popular that. Do a lot of sixties, as you'd expect. Up the stairs at the end of the corridor, turn left, second door on the right.'

The line went dead, as Rob looked at the door to his left and looked around again before walking over and pushing it fully open. There was a flight of stairs ahead, so he walked towards them and went up to the first floor. There, he found a door painted bright red, like a post box, with a sign on it that read *Rewinds*.

He stepped into a windowless room, lit only by a lamp on a desk that also held an old portable TV with a blank screen.

What's going on? he wondered, now wishing he'd gone straight home after work that afternoon. *In fact, I wish I hadn't gone out at all last night.*

The TV screen flickered into life, showing one of those old countdown clips they used to put on before TV shows and films played.

8...7...6...5...4...

There was no sound as a black-and-white film began to play; the title said *Liverpool: Gateway to the West* over a stylised picture of a docked ocean liner. The film showed an empty railway carriage chuntering along, overlooking the busy docks and the River Mersey; the overhead railway. The screen then flickered a little, and the next image showed a railway station sign of Canada Dock, followed by another for James Street. Finally, the same set of gates and building he'd seen in one of the old photos in the reception flashed up, after which the screen went off and came back on showing the countdown footage again, followed by the sound of a loud voice coming seemingly out of nowhere.

'You've got an hour,' it said.

Rob was plunged into absolute darkness. Feeling weightless and breathless, he began to panic as he strained his eyes for a sign of light, but there was nothing. Then, as quickly as it had started, he found himself back out in the open on what was now a much-changed street, with brick warehouses lining the road on both sides, and horse-drawn carts and old-fashioned lorries trundling along the cobbles.

He reached instinctively inside his coat pocket for his phone, doing a quick double check up and down before realising he wasn't in his own clothes, but rather an old overcoat, shirt, and suit. He looked down at his feet and saw he was wearing a pair of black leather boots, and upon touching the top of his head, he found he was wearing a flat cap.

It was raining heavily from the chilly, grey skies, but there was no wind. The air smelled of smoke and molasses.

What am I supposed to do? he thought quickly. *The film...the railway carriage and the two signs. What was the first one again? Canada Dock?*

He glanced around in an attempt at getting his bearings, and then turned left and walked for a few minutes towards the nearest junction; the street sign on the corner said Derby Road. He looked to his right and crossed the road, heading in what he assumed was the direction of Dock Road, finding it strange to not have to worry about cars and trucks while crossing, since the nearest wagon was two hundred yards away. He turned right again, this time down a side road, and there in front of him was the overhead railway, and a set of stairs that he assumed led to the platform.

Tickets, he thought, making his way over. *Could you bunk in the old days?*

He put his hand in his inside jacket pocket and pulled out a brown wallet. Inspecting its contents, he found a ticket with L.O.R printed on it, along with the station names Gladstone and James Street.

That'd work, wouldn't it? he thought, as he climbed the stairs up to the platform.

There was nobody else around; it was just him and a selection of adverts for long-forgotten brands of soap, sweets, and cigarettes. The rain was still coming down heavily, so he walked to the waiting room and took a seat on a wooden bench.

What did the voice say again? he thought. He didn't have a watch or phone, and he couldn't see a clock anywhere in the station. *An hour, was it? How long has it been now? ... Stay calm, just get to James Street and find the old building with the gates.*

A couple of men appeared on the platform opposite. Two of them stood together, talking loudly and smoking, another stood further away, reading an expertly folded newspaper. In the distance, a shop's horn sounded; he heard an approaching train clattering towards the station from the left, on his side. He stood up as it was coming to a halt and walked along the platform, peering into the carriages until he found an empty one and got in.

The train began lumbering its way along the raised line. He looked to his right and got a clear view of the ships in the dock, as well as the cranes and assorted goods that were arranged on the quayside. They arrived at the next stop, where a man in dirty overalls entered the carriage and sat down. Rob turned away, looking off to his left, and remarked to himself how busy it looked, this hive of activity amongst the bricks and iron and steel. He fell into a daze as the journey continued. The Liver Buildings loomed large in front of him; Pier Head, the station sign said.

Next stop, he thought, standing up and moving towards the doors. A couple of minutes later, the train came to a half and he stepped out onto the platform and headed smartly for the exit. It was busier here, noisy with conversations and the hum of a city going about its day. He went down the stairs and decided to walk along the Strand.

Right, he said to himself, *I need to find this place sharpish…big old building with gates,* he kept internally repeating this mantra as he walked along.

It felt strange to be where he'd always been, but to see it as it was in his great-grandfather's time. Thankfully, his instinct to walk that way had paid off, and he smirked to himself as he realised that he needn't have worried so much. A grand, palatial building stood in front of him, at once imposing and welcoming. He looked quickly for the gates and headed for them, not stopping to think about what he'd say if asked why he was there.

He approached the gates to the building, ready to walk in and see what happened, but as he stepped inside, it all went black. He was weightless again, in a vacuum. He blinked, waiting for the light, and when he looked up, he found himself back outside the office door.

It was sunny as he looked around before checking his pockets and pulling out his phone.

Derby Road, the map app said.

Delightful and Frightful
Siobhan Harte

Lights come up on stage to reveal a woman, Maenad, sitting in an inflatable dinghy. She looks dishevelled and distraught, with torn, bloody clothes and bloody scratches on her face and hands. Another woman, Heraclitus, enters, looking clean and well dressed.

Maenad: What can we talk about now?
Heraclitus: Food.
M: No. Not again. I can't. Sticky toffee pudding and custard, fish and chips, steak pie.
H: *(empathetically)* Vegan burgers and salad, tomato soup.
M: Hot buttered crumpets and toast and cups of tea. Oh god, I'm so thirsty, I'd kill for a cup of tea.
(H gives M a filthy look)
M: If I've ever been horrid, you do know I didn't mean it. *(mutters)* I'm sorry.
H: Easy to say now. Hmm! You know what you did!
M: *(Rocks a little, wiping her mouth)* Please. Let's put the past behind us. We can't change a thing now. You can't blame me. I know you were going to do the same thing. It's only that I got there before you.
H: Really? Hmm. You think so? I actually never would

have believed you capable, Maenad. We've known each other for how long now?

M: It's about ten…

H: *(angry)* Thirteen, Maenad. It's thirteen years now.

M: *(looks around guiltily, her mood changes)* Oh yes, tick, tick, tick. Who do you think you are anyway? When I met you, you were in your ivory tower weren't you? Just waiting to be rescued. Dropping that long blonde plait out of the window over and over and letting any old Prince climb up it, weren't you? Who had to kiss that disgusting toad for you to get him off your back, eh?

H: Who broke into that cottage and rescued YOU when you got caged up by that older woman who kept giving you sweets? I told you she was a feeder and a wrong 'un, but did you listen? No. You always know best. In fact, if you weren't such a know it all and a bully, we wouldn't even be here, would we?

M: *(mouths)* A know it all and a bully…me?

H: Yeah. I wanted to wait for a few more months. But no. Princess Maenad has to have her holidays now. Right now. *(pauses)* Enjoying the sunshine yet?

M: I'm so hot. I feel really burnt. *(cries)*

H: I could've gone to prison, breaking into that cottage for you – I did it for you.

M: Okay, okay. *(cries)* It's probably me that's going to prison now anyway.

H: Oh god, I've had enough of this. I'm going. A four-hour flight cut rather painfully short I must say, followed by thirty six days with you? No. I'm going. *(slowly)* You're on your own.

M: No. No please, Heraclitus. Heraclitus, please don't leave me here. I can't stand it without you. Don't go over there, please stay, please, you're gonna drown. *(She sobs, face in hands as H walks slowly backwards off stage)*

(Pause as M recovers herself and addresses the audience)

M: I didn't want to. I wasn't in my right mind, I promise you. And stop judging me – all of you, you'd have done the same. I know you would. *(pause)* It was horrible. Truly, truly horrible. I mean, any human would be really. But she was my friend, a real friend. The worst bit, aside from my nails ripping into her flesh, and the blood, oh god, so much blood. The worst bit – thirteen hours later, I heard the helicopter. If I'd waited just thirteen hours more – she would have been rescued too.

Hollywood Platinum Star
Siobhan Harte

An elderly woman is sitting in an armchair in the day room of a care home. She has carefully coiffed and sprayed platinum blond hair, her makeup is heavy; she wears a day dress, tan tights, and warm slippers, but has an air of glamour and 'otherness' about her. She looks up as though she finally has somebody to speak to.

You wanna know about my life? I'll tell you. They were all there of course – Gene Kelly, Jack Lemmon – Oh he was such fun! *(suggestive)* Okay, I'll admit it, I was a little jealous of Rita Hayworth – she was breathtaking, and God, that girl could dance! Never Marilyn though – she was a terrible actress, and all that breathing. Okay, she was beautiful…really beautiful, but I can tell you after a long hot day in the studio – I could have slapped her. And all the men would swarm around her like flies on shit – and she would just *(inhales and exhales)* …breathe. I guess it says more about then men than it does about her. God, I could see how vulnerable she was, they kind of ripped her apart you know. I guess I could have helped her more, but I was too busy trying to get the director to look at me and not her. My god, the things I had to do in that town just to get a fuckin' audition. And once it starts, there's no getting away from it.

She briefly pauses, looking down and shaking her head before inhaling and resuming.

But I don't think of that. I wanted to be in the movies so bad. From the first time I saw Bette Davis onscreen. Whatever happened to Baby Jane?

She rises. (singing) I'm sending a letter to Daddy, the address is heaven above.

She chuckles as she remembers.

My god I looked up to that woman. I was forever knocking on her changing room door, bringing her things I thought she might like; never forgetting her cigarettes of course. God, I used to worry about how much she smoked. Of course, she got old, nearly as old as I am now. Then they don't want you. Well, they do, but ya go from leading lady and more adoration than is healthy…

God, I remember this guy once. He was arrested thirteen times for standing on my lawn at night and staring up at my window with a pair of binoculars. I mean it wasn't even a crime back then but ya know, 'cause of who I am and all, the cops used to come out just to get a look at me – in the end they were all warned to stop asking me for my signature and taking stones and shit off my lawn. Anyway, yeah. Ya go from leading lady and dozens of beautiful dresses, to they put you in a chair by the fire for an hour just so you can say: 'Don't worry, darling, Grandma will always love you' to some little brat whose salary is thirteen times more than what you're earning. So, I mean, you take it because the alternative is back on the road to the theatre.

She pauses. Shakes her head and shrugs.

Well, that's Hollywood for you. I could tell you so many stories. Is that it? Is that all you want?

She walks across the stage, pointing her walking stick offstage.

Oh, you better not listen to her. There's exactly nothing wrong with me. Every day. Every day she comes along here: 'Oh, come on now, young lady. How's our star this morning?'

Fuck you. I'm an old lady not a young lady and I WAS a star. You wouldn't know class if it came and bit you on the ass, bitch. This fuckin' place. It's the same every single day. I've got eighty-year-old men trying to feel me up – they remember me from the movies you know. And the food. I'd rather eat my own shit. Some days I do and I wipe it on the walls, and boy do I have a laugh watching these bitches trying to clean it off.

Fuckin' jelly and cheap ice cream. I'm not a fuckin' baby you know.

She pauses and controls her anger, sitting back in her chair.

Yeah, I suppose you can come back next week and see if I feel like speaking to you again. I guess you'll have to wait and see, it'll be a nice surprise for ya won't it. Or maybe not.

She settles back in her armchair, pulling her pashmina around her shoulders, and waves her hand dismissively at the audience with her eyes shut.

Now fuck off.

Lights down. The End.

Capture
Sharon Hayes

I look up and he's there
I look down and he's gone
I can't see
He's not there

I look at my feet
Blistered and torn
Looking up makes it too real
Looking down, he's not there

I can't think of my journey, how I got here and when
He's moving around
I take a breath and it hurts – hurts the silence.
I look up, he's there

He whispers, his breath hanging there for me to smell
I'm not scared anymore
If I look up, he's gone
But then, so am I…

Alone
Sharon Hayes

How can I feel so alone?
Laughter, music...
How do I feel so alone?
Then I see you
and I won't be.

Shoelace
Sharon Hayes

He ties one shoelace
Leaves one undone
Is that today's plan?
Is that how he'll get noticed?
'Be careful, you'll trip.'
Ah, so that's how he'll get noticed
Someone cared
Then, they were gone.

Wait
Sharon Hayes

Is it hard for you
to pull the wall down?
Frightened it will make a noise
Disturbing the silence
Is it hard for you
to know what's on the other side?
Should I be there, on that other side?
Will you walk until the bricks become sand?
Is it hard for you
to tell me if I should wait?

Her
Iain Hendrie

Her hair is curly and frizzy
Her heart is made of gold
Our wedding night nuptials were amazing
My heart beats with joy when I see her smile
And my soul weeps when
I don't meet her expectations

I love her

The Mother of my children
An Auntie to my sisters kids
A stanchion to stop me falling

Have I mentioned I love her?

She means the world to me.
She means the universe to me.
She means more than words can say

I really do love her.

Good Enough for Who?
Jennifer Hughes

He said I wasn't good enough; her father told her, too.
Stuffed barrel of words, endless loop.
Too large, too plump, too foreign, too much…
Rammed into her brain – not good enough for you.

Sunken, sombre eyes, a story dug deep in her forgotten mind.
He said she wasn't good enough, but good enough for who?

Three girls she raised alone, with love, attention and dedication.
Still, it wasn't good enough.
Too round, too harsh, too struct…
Not good enough as a mum, wife, or office manager, but am I good enough for you?

Three girls, all unique, individual and fierce.
Mum's twinkle in their eyes.
Each an image of her, right to the end of her button nose.
Two blonde, one brunette, battling and raging in the wild.

Into the fire and wind, the three flew.
Adventure awaits, but Mum is always at home for you.
Standing tall, their mother's story etched into their wings.
She took her pen, gripped it tight and wrote her narrative again.

Woolf's whispers of finding a pen, a room, a book, some space…
Words scrawl the page, winding, twisting, and flowing freely for the first time.
Learning to be good enough.
Her story rewritten again.

We Are Liverpool
Jennifer Hughes

We are Liverpool.
This is home, born and bred.
Starting in Bottle.
The Strand, shoe shops, butchers, and McDonald's with Mum and sister.
We grew up.
I moved away.
It drew me back.

We are Liverpool.
Tap! Tap! Tap!
Heavy footsteps hammering around Sefton Park for the Spring 10K.
People running for charity – for one another.
For Alder Hey Children's Hospital.
They saved my sister when she was six.
Right here in our Liverpool, caring for our kids.

We are Liverpool.
Lark Lane, food and bars.
Arts and students.
Everywhere around.
Red or Blue?
Whether it's Derby Day or elections, we're choosing

either way.
We're voting with our hearts, voting for each other.
Voting for our rights.
For better lives for one another.
For the community.
But my neighbour's little girl was shot.
Nine years old.
Gangs, crime, rats and ruin.

We are Liverpool.
Drag them out of our city.
Neighbours, communities.
We fight for one another.
Dark, sinister; empty can of Carling twatted down the road.
All dressed head-to-toe in black, together in gangs.
Dark stares bringing fear.

We are Liverpool.
No place in this community.
The place that drew me back.
Home.

Albert's Dilemma
Michael Inniss

It was the silence that was strange. A deathly silence! And although death was no stranger to the general population, its invisibility hung in the atmosphere filling the men and women with a dread which they had never experienced. It was a stark reminder of the inevitability of the cessation of life.

This was no more apparent to anyone than Albert Jones as the ambulance drew up to take his wife, Margaret, to the local hospital. They had been married for 52 years and she had never really been ill. But now she was experiencing chest pains and Albert thought it was probably the best thing he could do by ringing for the ambulance.

Margaret, however, did not want to go to the hospital. She told him that it was a dangerous place at the moment as there was this dreadful virus circulating and people were dying in the hospitals even members of the staff. Albert sought to comfort her. 'You will be alright. You will be in a different ward,' he told her soothingly.

Albert accompanied her to the hospital. They went through the necessary procedure and Margaret was admitted. Four days later Albert received a call from the hospital asking him to come in as Margaret's condition had worsened. Albert dressed hurriedly while dialling for a taxi.

On arrival at the hospital Ward, he met the senior nurse. She explained to him that unfortunately Margaret had contracted the Corona virus and had passed away. 'How could that be possible?' Albert asked. 'She came in with heart problems and placed in a separate ward.' The nurse tried her best to explain. A doctor was then summoned and he, too, attempted to explain to him the circumstances of Margaret's demise. But Albert remained unconvinced.

About two hours later, Albert arrived home. He stood outside and looked around. There was no one in sight as he walked hesitatingly up the path, fished the keys from his pocket and entered the house. This is all a dream, he thought. Margaret will be inside waiting for him. He opened the living room door tentatively, looked inside but there was no Margaret. The full realisation then came home to him. He reeled slightly and held on to the settee.

Recovering, minutes later, Albert sat on the settee. 'What now?' he mused. They had talked jokingly about who would be the first to go without seriously confronting the possibility. Presently, however, Albert had to face the reality that Margaret had gone before him. Memories flooded like that of a drowning man. They led a sheltered life, had no real friends. Now there was no one to inform of her passing; no family members. Margaret was an only child and he sighed as he recalled how his two siblings had both passed away.

Albert rose from the settee and wandered into the kitchen. Robotically, he switched on the kettle and searched for his favourite mug. Where did she put it? She was always moving things. And in desperation he began smashing everything that he could lay his hands on. Finally, as his rage subsided, he sat down. A feeling of guilt overwhelmed him as his thoughts wandered to all the places, all the things they had done together. 'Soul mates, we are', he always joked. After their marriage, they decided that they would not have any children. In low-paid jobs, the thought of rearing children in near poverty terrified them. Therefore, they remained childless. Sadly, there was now no one but himself to mourn Margaret's passing; there was no other person to attend her funeral.

Albert looked around him and surveyed the myriad of broken articles. Among the wreckage was Margaret's cherished Royal Doulton teapot. And this made him recall that she did not want to go to the hospital; she told him about the virus and that she was afraid. He licked his lips, tasted the saltiness of his tears and cried inconsolably. He whispered through his tears, 'I am so sorry my love. It should not have happened this way. No hugs. No kisses. No last goodbyes. However, Albert knew immediately what would end his torment. He went to the medicine cabinet in the bathroom, took out the boxes of pain killers and strolled into the kitchen. Methodically, he emptied the boxes of tablets inside the sole remaining mug while humming Margaret's favourite tune, 'Delilah'. He then poured a generous shot of his favourite Irish whiskey into the mug, added some water from the kettle and stirred the toxic cocktail. 'I'll be seeing you soon, Marge' he whispered.

Albert and Margaret were never religious. They were married at a Registry Office. Therefore, there were no prayers to offer; no one to ask for forgiveness. He picked up the mug and cupped it in his hands. It was piping hot. This gave him time to reflect on what had brought him to this point. This Corona epidemic, which they had learned about on the TV and which they thought did not really affect them. It seemed like something from the Biblical films with plagues and pestilence. All he knew was they received Government letters which told them to stay indoors. 'Lockdown', they called it. They were 'over 70 and vulnerable'. Margaret had explained to him that the advice was for their safety. So they stayed indoors. 'Where was that safety now, eh?' He asked himself.

Albert's tears no longer flowed as he once again placed the mug to his lips. He was about to take a sip when a voice, out of nowhere, came to him, 'What are you doing you silly old bugger?' It was Margaret's voice. Albert recoiled in horror. The mug fell from his hands and shattered on the wooden floor spilling the contents over his shoes.

'Margaret, is that you?' he asked in an ethereal voice.

His head swivelled frantically, searching for the source of the voice. He was shaking violently. There was no one visible. No apparition of Margaret. 'What the hell . . .' he whispered. He was totally confused. It took several minutes for Albert to calm down. He looked on the floor at the broken mug. It was Margaret's: the one with the picture of the Blackpool tower. And as he gazed at the fragments of the broken tower an aura of tranquillity and sadness surrounded him. She had to have the last word, he thought.

2021: Eighteen months after Margaret's passing the Corona pandemic, which had decimated millions of the world population, had abated. Seemingly, the mass inoculation of the public had the desirable effect but there were still reports in parts of the country that variants of the disease were prevalent. Members of the public were still wearing masks. Restrictions, placed by the Government in the early days, had now been lifted and travelling worldwide had resumed. A sense of normality prevailed...

Presently, Albert stood at Margaret's graveside,

holding a small floral cross. He wore his wedding suit which was totally unfashionable and hung loosely on his emaciated body. He shifted nervously. It was the third time that he had visited the grave because of the 'Lockdown' He was also unable to travel because of the difficulty with public transport. Today, however, he was on a double mission of contrition and confession. He bowed, whispered a prayer, and placed the Cross on the grave. 'Well, Marge', he began, 'everything is slowly changing. However, I am not managing very well. It has been disastrous without you… I couldn't work either the washing machine or the oven. I miss you so much, Marge. The mail man, Jack, helped me. He sorted everything out for me… He has been a godsend…

'Speaking of God, Marge, I went to church. It felt nice and peaceful as I said a prayer for you. Yes, me, praying. And you know what, since then I have been going every Sunday. Strangely, I feel more of my old self and I have come to terms with your passing. I now know that things happen in our lives over which we have no control and death is one of them. So, now I pray that you will rest in peace until that wonderful day when we meet again. God bless!

Thankful!
Michael Inniss

Today, I hanker for the old days in the pub
The laughter, the banter, the general hubbub
Tots of whisky, pints of ale.
The old sovereignty of the species male.
I yearn for the old days with my mates
No worries about mortgage payments or rates.
Recently, I ventured in the city to visit a pub
It was a tenner to enter, it was not a club
I stood at the bar nursing my bottle of Bud lager
Which had, I may add, cost me a fiver
To me, it all seemed so very strange
Watching the customers not counting their change
We knew the prices of all the beers
Rum, vodka, gin and the liquors
'Hey, love, there's a sixpence less,'
Counting the coins, we stood no mess
'Sorry, love,' as she placed the coin on the bar
'It's alright, place it in the jar.'
She'll place the tanner in the glass on the shelf
Sharing the spoils later with the staff and herself
I watch the punters paying for their bevvy
With their phones, not with money.
It would not have surprised me
If they had paid in crypto currency

From the Ashes

The youngsters stood with their drinks in their hands
No tables, no chairs, they all had to stand
Shoulder to shoulder they dance
Shaking their stiff bodies as if in a trance.
In short sleeves the lads chose to wear
Never mind it was in the middle of winter
Mini skirts, off the shoulder, the order of the day
Made me wonder if it was the middle of May.
I do not wish to cause any offence
But where there is no feeling, there is no sense.
I just stood at the bar watching in awe
At the names of the drinks, ordered by the score
Black Russian, white lady, mai tai, daiquiri,
pina colada, mojito, and dark and stormy.
At ten pounds a go I had to ponder
Are these kids all off their rocker.
These ridiculous prices did not seem to matter
I tell you what, it made my eyes water.
The crowd was now getting boisterous
Arguing and shouting, very vociferous
It was the moment I dread
When the drinks went to their head
The lads were all pushing and swearing
I had visions of knives appearing.
So I said to myself, head for the exit
Time to get out of this veritable snake pit.
Then I yearned for the old days even more

There was no fighting and gore
We old chaps sat round the table on chairs
Discussing events of bygone years
Sports and politics were the order of the day
We sipped our ale and belched without dismay.
Waitress service, stools by the bar
You ordered your drinks without going far
A bottle of Guinness, a Mackie and halves of Mild
No fancy titles and spending wild.
We sat around the table telling our jokes
About the Scots, Welsh and Irish, there was no woke
There was the ability to laugh at ourselves
Or for that matter, anyone else.
With bellies full of beer and all in good cheer
We waited for the vendor to appear
Making his way through the throng
Will be the lad making his round
Crying 'potted shrimps, mussels, and cockles'
(Sorry, no caviar, sushi, and truffles)
It may appear to some it was not gastronomic
But we were before our time. They were organic!
Then there were pork scratchings and packet of nuts
Together with pickled eggs we filled our guts
A bobby would always make an appearance
Looking for under-age drinkers or some other pretence.
He would take off his helmet, stand in the corner

The Manager then sidled and slipped him a beer
Out will go the 'scallies' and 'divvies'
Taking no chance with one of the bizzies.
Then the Sally Army crew will pass by
Selling their issues of the 'War Cry'
There was always 'small change' for the Army without guns
And you kept some back for the visit of the Nuns.
The pubs, you see, were part of the community
And we were all glad to give to charity
Well, not all, as you will hear the local wag
Shouting at someone, 'You bloody minge bag',
Yes, we old timers knew how to behave
Although among us there was always the odd knave.

Then the sound of the bell brought unease
As the manager's cry followed, 'Last Orders, please'
There was no rush to the bar for another jar
No, we have had enough by far.
Off to the Gents with heads held erect
Showing each other a mark of respect
No looks left, right, up and down
To do so would create a mighty frown.
Please remember, it was not just a haven for men
Let's not forget the singing of the women
Now don't get me wrong

Writing on the Wall

It was not the Pale Ale and Stout that brought on the song.
We sang the old music hall favourites
And others that were at one time 'hits'.
They were those from down memory lane
About bombs, blackouts and aeroplane
And among those old lilts was the refrain
Vera Lynn's 'We'll Meet Again'
'I'll be Seeing You' and 'White Cliffs of Dover'
Marie Lloyd songs and Harry Lauder
And those made famous by Formby and Askey
Never mind if they were sung off key.
Then the dreaded bell and shout from the Manager,
'Drink up please,' in a bellowed but decent manner.
We'll stagger out singing but with good behaviour
Unless you want a ride in the Black Maria.
Yes, it was all so different in our day
Therefore, we look back pining for the old way.
However, in a more sombre moment
I dwell on the facts of this new advent.
We are at a more sedentary age,
And cannot afford to be consumed with rage.
No longer can we ignore this sea of change,
Despite the actuality that it all seems strange.
We, elderly, now face a phenomenal stage in life
But it does not have to be trouble and strife.
Past, Present, Future: this Holy Trinity

From the Ashes

Is the framework of a boundless eternity.
Let's accept that the change is not apocalyptical,
Grow in stature and be less hypercritical.
We can make drastic changes at this stage,
Enjoy the scent of flowers: lavender and sage
Joys of nature, ignored by so many
Can no longer be subliminal, just heavenly.
Three score and ten? It was an age celebrated
By Biblical fathers and others so fated.
They were quite contented
With an age not lamented.
Now listen fellow 'oldies' don't make a fuss
Let's put all this perceived adversity behind us.
Do not despair, shed not a tear
Just be glad that we are still here.

PINK GUMS
Caitlin Jones

I roll over again, burying my face in the pillow. I'm not ready. I don't want to leave. Not now. Not today. My phone alarm rings for the millionth time. That fucking noise. I hate it. I feel around the bed, where is it? The ringing becomes intolerable as I unearth it from the bedcovers.

Snooze.

Sorted.

Wait, did that say 3:15? Fuck. Not just fuck as in, fuck I've slept in but fuck as in: I'm fucking late.

The one day I've got to be somewhere, I think, as I frantically look round my room for clothes that say 'I'm sane! I'm just a functioning member of society, like everyone else.' After looking round my room for more than a minute I realise, I don't own clothes like that. And all my decent stuff is in the wash. Well, waiting to be washed. At this point, the basket is more like a general target area. My phone rings again. This time, not an alarm but my dad. I answer. Which is rare.

'I fucking told you!'

So it begins. I light one of the stubbed out ciggie's in the ashtray and settle in.

'Me and your mum work our arses off, we've paid for 3 sessions for you to sort your head out and I've just got a call off the woman saying you haven't even shown up!'

When he gets like this, I just throw him on loudspeaker and then mute, so I carry on doing whatever I was doing, while he carries on. Easier that way.

'Eighty quid a week, do you think I've got that money? Do you think your mum's got that kind of money?'

I could say no, which would be true. Or I could say yes and bring up how he's more annoyed that the 80 quid a week for three weeks is cutting into his bevvy money. But today's about growth and change. I decide to avoid conflict and say nothing.

'Do you? Do you?! Are you even listening? I know you think…'

To be honest, background pent up anger is quite soothing. Easy to block out. I pick up some jeans. There's a bit of dried blood on the knees from where I fell over the other night. Great first date. Although I fear I'm getting to that age where my antics aren't a funny story to tell my friends about. It's getting sad. I can see that. Oh no! Am I losing my ability to be the fun, free-spirited girl you go out with and don't know or care where you'll end up? It's not fun anymore though. I'd change fun, to low mood and free-spirited, to reckless.

And girl to woman.

'… it's a fucking joke. You've got no respect …'

I check the pockets while he continues. There's a bus ticket scrunched up. Suddenly a wave of optimism pours over me. I think this could be the bag of lemo we lost the other night. Please, let this be the bag. I unwrap the ticket ever so carefully, ready to catch any bits that might fall on the floor. Fucking, get in! It's there! I really do feel a genuine happiness with my find. The sort of happiness I imagine people feel when they hear their song on the radio or when their kid got an award for not being a little shit in school. It's such a heart-warming feeling. He's still banging on. I hear him say he's asked her to push it back until her next free slot which is 4:30.

I hold the bag up to the light and give it a shake. Fair bit left. I lock my phone and begin to rack. I can still hear him on the other end. Whatever makes him feel better.

'Why have you got to be like this?! Why?! I know you didn't have a perfect life, but I don't understand – I put my neck on the line for you time and time again. I have your back in front of your mum, your nan and still all you do is throw it back in my face.'

I have a line off the phone and unmute him. I'm going to try and take a calm approach.

'Dad. I'm sorry,' I say, but even I know it doesn't sound genuine. What the fuck is wrong with me? I *mean* it. I *am* sorry. But I already know he won't think of it as a sincere apology. Sorry gets flung about so much, the word has lost all value.

'Oh, don't start this now. You're not sorry. You think money comes and goes. We can see you're struggling and the wait for TalkLiverpool was months long, so I've paid for this for you as a favour…'

Fucking hell, same shit different day. I go to the bathroom. I should probably brush my teeth. As daunting as that sounds, yeah, I should probably tick that off my list. I pull the light which hangs next to the mirror. Suddenly, I'm face to face with myself. First time in about two days. I hate mirrors. I don't know what it is. These last few months, I just … I look older. Decrepit. This is what I meant by "not that cute" before. Be a mess, yeah! But just … try not to look like one is what I've learned these last few years. I haven't taken any care of myself. My eyes, they're dull, tired but wide. My nose, it bleeds more often than not nowadays. My mouth, it hurts. My teeth are fucked. My arms and hands, they don't look like mine anymore, and my ears, well, if we're going to do all the senses, they constantly feel like they need to pop. Hearing clearly is a luxury. I can't remember the last time I didn't have to ask someone to repeat what they said. Why have I done this to myself? As I brush my teeth, my gums start to bleed. I should probably make a dentist appointment.

Dad's still going on, I can hear him starting to calm down. His voice is in a softer tone now. I think he's started to turn inward. We're at the self-reflection part of the argument.

'You know, babe, I never dealt with a lot of stuff that I went through with your nan and grandad or whatever ...' I note how he brushes over his chequered past. 'And you don't want to end up like me, do you?'

The answer is no. No, of course I don't. However, I do want another line.

'Well ... there's not much more I can say. Just go. Please. You've got an hour to get there.' He trails off. Fucking hell. I think for a moment. Maybe I am just being a dickhead lately.

We say bye. He lets me know he put some bus fare in my account and then the call cuts off. Silence. It's weird living by yourself in moments like this. I don't really know what to do with myself. Listen to music? I'm not too sure what music I like anymore. I can't think of a song. I can't think of a film. I look around my living room, looking for something to catch my eye. It's been such a long week. I've finished the bag I found in my jeans and now, I'm stagnant.

My brain is too loud. How can everything else around me be so still and so silent? There's so much going through my mind, I don't know how to unpack it all. I check my phone for some alcohol delivery app. So many random cards on my phone. One of them has got to work. My ex, he blocked the card. That's how I know it's over. Cut off completely. See what I mean? These antics, they aren't that cute anymore.

Don't think about it.

Someone's got to have 30 quid at least. It's only a bottle of JD and Coke. I just start clicking cards at this point.

This card has insufficient funds. This card has insufficient funds. This card has insufficient funds. This card has insufficient funds. This card has insufficient funds. This card has insufficient funds.

I see.

There's one more option, but I really hate asking her for money. I know she's skint. And we both know when I say 'I'll send you it when my UC comes in' I'm lying. But ... I really want a drink.

I ring her phone.

'Mum?'

'Hi.' She sounds drained as always. But sometimes this is good, sometimes she's too tired to argue.

'How are you?'

'What do you want?'

Okay, so we're doing this. 'I was just wondering if I could lend some money until my UC comes in—'

'What for?'

'I just need to pay a bill and also, get some food in.'

Not a complete lie.

She sighs. I feel bad. I do. It takes her minute to build up the energy to reply.

'How much do you need?'

'Fort— no sorry fifty pounds ...?'

I took a risk there. She never has fifty quid. She sighs again. The wait is killing me.

'Go on. I'll send it now.' She's so stern. What is up with her?

'Thanks mum, love y—'

She's already gone. I immediately check my online banking. Still £4 from the money my dad sent me. I should've said £56 instead of £50. After a minute or two I see she's sent it. Well, that's one problem fixed. I check the time. I've got 30 minutes. I suppose I could walk there and just pick up a bevvy on the way. Maybe not a good first impression to show up to therapy with a bag full of ale. Or there's that gig tonight. I don't know if I'm ready for social interaction yet. I haven't replied to anyone in over three and a half weeks. I don't know what to say. I think I'm done saying things. I've said too much.

I've managed to make a one skinner out of some dust in the grinder and just what residue is on the table. I light it and then catch a look at myself in the broken mirror next to the TV. Broken because of me. I think this isolation/hermit period I've been in has been pretty beneficial. I mean people say you need friends, and you do. But this level of introspection is unmatched. I obviously smashed the mirror because I don't want to look at myself! I hate myself! And everything I do is—.

The phone rings again. This time it's my friend. I should probably answer. I just watch it instead. I don't know what to say. I've got nothing to say. 'Hiii, I'm sorry I've not been answering, I just had a mad week the other week and ...yeah.' I should wear that on a T-shirt. The phone stops ringing and then I get a text.

'I MISS YOU!! WHERE HAVE YOU GONE?!'

It makes me smile. I have really good friends. I want to text back, but I'm stuck to the couch. The spliff feels like it's just sunk into the sides of my fingers. I don't want to move. I take a deep pull and exhale. I've got 20 minutes.

Time to go.

I can feel myself starting to talk myself out of going. I give myself a few options. Either go the cashpoint, get the money out and then bolt it down Prinny. Get the 50 out and then get the 27 towards L1. Or taxi there, so I don't run the risk of bumping into anyone on the walk. My brain is overwhelmed with the options. I think for a minute as I get my shoes on. Could just get a 30s of lemo and then 20 on bevvy?

Okay. It's decided. Great plan. Perhaps I don't need therapy after all?

Time
John Kelly

When we're born, we have all of it
All the time in the world
Time to spend
Time to waste
Time to kill
Time…

It becomes more important to us
More pressing
We haven't got the time
It flies
Time…

As life goes on, it runs out
Kids have far too much of it to fill
Parents never have enough of it
Time…

It can never be bought
It's how we spend it that matters
Time…

Once it's gone, it's never coming back
Time…

You
Rikki Kielle

I am sorry for everything I have said and done
Out of fear, out of line, out from the past
Treating you like shit, as if you were there
Breaking & grinding & tearing
Those debts lie on other's shoulders
with their lies, their hate, their fears

But that doesn't give me the right,
To break, to take, to steal.
You are my everything.
My heart, my life, my soul.

You show me the way
to live, to feel, to love.
You opened my eyes, and now I can see
The wonder, the beauty, the light.

The unstoppable force meets the immovable object
caught up in your momentum
we clash, we dance, we spin

You tore down my defences,
piece by piece by bloody piece
Patience was never your virtue,

yet you gave me your everything.

I have taken & taken & taken
But now it's my time to give
Because to you, I owe everything
And now I hold you up on my shoulders
To give you the support, the love you need.

You lifted the veil of my darkest delusion
And now I have only one conclusion,
The light at the end of the tunnel
is hope.

The Log Cabin
Anne Lunt

Big wooden house so big and WOW!
Inside it's amazing,
Not what we thought,
Looking out of the window
There's a red robin, a tree,
The views are so beautiful,
And magical too,
The boys love it so much,
With the sun in the morning,
The moon in the night,
The colours in the sky,
Shining upon the lake,
Our holidays only just begun,
And how we love it here,
Oh, it's our last day,
And that red robin's back again.

Mavis and Ted

Anne Lunt

Here is a man and wife, Mavis and Ted, going out together for afternoon tea. It's their 50th Anniversary.

'You walk on my right, dear. We don't want any accident now, do we?' he says, and slowly they walk.

Ted whistles their favourite song. They look so happy together. They arrive at the Old Tearoom and Ted pulled Mavis out of her chair so she could sit down.

'Thank you, dear. It's lovely in here, isn't it, Ted? Just like the one when we were young.'

'Yes, Mavis. It's lovely. It takes me back to when I was twenty and you were eighteen.'

They had ham and tuna sandwiches, then jam and cream scones, then a pot of tea each.

'What a lovely day it's been,' Mavis said, 'I've really enjoyed myself. Have you enjoyed yourself, Ted?'

Ted replied, 'I really have, my dear, but it's not finished yet.'

He looked towards one of the tearoom staff and nodded. 'Happy Anniversary, dear.' They brought a beautiful big bouquet of flowers over to Mavis.

'How lovely, my favourite roses, freesias and gypsy grass. Thank you so much, Ted! Happy 50th Anniversary!'

Have You Ever?
Matthew Lunt

Have you ever seen a cow riding a cloud?
Have you ever seen an ant lifting a rocket up?
Have you ever seen a pig eating himself?
Have you ever seen a pencil eating a nettle?
Have you ever seen a spider drinking cider?
Have you ever seen a crocodile making an army base?
Have you ever seen a chicken eating chicken nuggets?
Have you ever seen a frog eating a log?

Bleeding Hearts
Jennifer McAlister

It had been a long time since I last entered Camelot's castle. On our arrival, I hypnotised the king's guards to permit us entry. I was technically still a Knight of the Round Table, although news of my condition had spread across all the realms, including to the far-reaches of Camelot, so I was hardly expecting a jubilant reception.

The laments of the orchestra resonated from the Great Hall; all those theatrics from him, a tad over-dramatic even by my standards. Memories of a youth spent roaming these hallowed halls still echoed in my memory, and the sombre atmosphere aside, the castle had changed little since I was last there. The old suits of armour and tapestries still adorned the long hallways; I had gazed longingly at them in my childhood, imagining my father's noble feats and longing to fight by his side, but I came to realise that such lavish displays were nothing more than us gloating about our heritage. Still, despite how misled the Camelotian's might have been, it was hard to blame them for falling for the falsehoods of their spineless king.

I myself was once far from immune to them all.

As we drew closer to my father's chamber, the door opened before us. Jermaine turned white and began searching for a way to conceal our presence.

'Now, there's hardly a need for that,' I said, breathlessly amused.

Emerging from the room within was the ever-stern Guinevere, wearing her usual frown of discontent.

My father has his own dragon guarding the tower, I thought.

Guinevere hadn't changed at all during my long absence, her appearance still eclipsed by a pointy crooked nose; contoured by her dishevelled, overgrown brunette hair; and those petrifying, icy, harlequin-green eyes, which would have made even the most fearsome beast flee in cowardice. That's without mentioning the rather large wart on her chin, big enough to have its own standing in my father's court.

I've met old crones sultrier than she, I thought.

Considering she was the queen of the most powerful kingdom in all the realms, one couldn't help but wonder why she hadn't sought to beautify her appearance, especially when she had the legendary power of the oldest and most magnificent wizard at her back and call.

Now, reader, don't be mistaken by my harsh description; it isn't for the sake of being condescending. Her unsightly appearance aside, her demeanour was equally wicked. The woman held me in undisguised contempt while I was growing up, never mincing her harsh words or missing an opportunity to berate me for even the most innocent childish mistakes. My father wasn't the most affectionate parent, either, though at least he was not as cruel, so it was a mystery to me as to why he chose her.

True love, if you could have called it that, was indeed a blind mistress.

'Lord Jophiel, finally come to visit your father in his late hour, I see,' she said by way of greeting.

I cringed to hear a name I hadn't been called in many years. It repulsed me, and I was all too eager to relinquish it upon my death. Jeremaine had always called me Josef, a name I found much more fitting.

'Guinevere,' I said, taking her hand and kissing it. 'Still using the beauty treatments of swing, I see? A displeasure as always.'

Being a monster didn't excuse me from being polite, though I did reserve the right to deem when and where it was appropriate. The look on her face brought on a mocking smile that my lips were only too willing to abide.

'Say your goodbyes and leave,' she spat, snatching her hand away. 'You are not welcome here, and if you are not gone by sunrise, you can be certain that you shan't awaken from your unnatural slumber. If there are any murders during the night, no matter peasant or noble, I will hold you and your friend here personally accountable. I will strip your knighthood upon your father's final breath, for it is only he whom insists upon upholding your honour.' She cracked the door and announced my presence. 'Arthur, your son is here.'

She never tried to hide the scorn in her voice whenever she forced my name from her lips, undead or otherwise.

'Send him in,' a faint voice wheezed in the gloom.

She bid us adieu, leaving to do whatever it was she did; perhaps to trim her nose hair before a nightcap.

'You should show your mother some respect,' Jeremaine whispered in my ear as she left.

'Oh, misguided Jeremaine,' I laughed, caressing his arm and flicking his fringe away from his face, whilst deliberately making no effort to conceal my words. 'She's no mother of mine!'

We entered His Majesty's chamber to find the old man rotting away in his bed. The inconsolable old wizard knelt at his bedside, looking more youthful than one might expect.

'This is too soon,' Merlin wept. 'You weren't meant to die this way, I've seen it!'

Magic wielders age slower than your average mortal, and some folktales claimed him to be thousands of years old. Whatever the case, he appeared younger than even I, who died at twenty-four.

'Now, now, Merlin,' I sneered, prompting him to

spring up from my father's bedside, frantic at my intrusion. 'You more than anyone should know that things aren't always the way they appear. Mourning doesn't become you, and besides, my father isn't even dead yet.'

'Begone, Jophiel,' he said. 'Your father doesn't need a foul demon pestering him on his deathbed!'

I hissed, on guard and ready to pounce. I would have taken great pleasure in ending the wizard, with any meaningful attachment I felt to him having disappeared once I discovered the deceptive nature of magic for myself.

'It's alright, Merlin,' my father said faintly.

My father, ladies and gentlemen – and those of you whom are neither – always sucking the joy out of any scene.

'Leave me to speak with my son,' the king croaked. 'I can handle his newly-found countenance unattended.'

'As you wish, sire,' Merlin acquiesced, taking his leave with a bow whilst sending a glare of distrust my way, before pausing to spout his usual drivel to my companion. 'Heed my words, friend of the beast. Beware the serpent, for even friendship won't spare you from its venomous bite.'

'I, for one, certainly do not miss his fatuous riddles,' I remarked to Jeremaine, as the door finally closed behind the departing wizard.

'Son, I hoped you'd come,' my father wheezed.

Mortals are so fragile and susceptible to many ills, magical or otherwise, regardless of whether they have unfinished business on this earth. Death is always inevitable, and occasionally she enjoys a helping hand. I myself have caused many deaths in my time, leaving me to wonder what awaited me beyond the sunset of mortal life.

'Does my condition not offend His Majesty?' I asked, since if offended everyone else.

'Your condition does not matter to me,' he answered. 'All that matters is you're here now.'

'And why does that concern you now? You never sought to find what became of me, nor did you protect me from your wench during my youth.'

'It matters because you're my son,' he coughed. 'I have many regrets in my life, and how you were treated is one of them.'

It was too little, too late for this fruitless sentiment.

'And so you should,' I said coldly. 'I was the spawn of an act of revenge, all because your wife had an affair with your best friend. Is it any wonder I turned out to be the monster that haunts people's nightmares?'

'No, it's no wonder. Life didn't show you the kindness you were due, an innocent downtrodden by circumstances beyond his control. It is for that reason I am hoping to make amends now, whilst I still have the chance.'

Stake me here and now and be done with it, I thought. *Save me from the abridged lament of my life.*

'And pray tell, dear father,' I said.

For once, I'm not the only dead man in the room, I thought.

'How do you amend the irreparable?'

He reached for his sword on his bedside table, attached to his hand until the very end.

'Your inheritance,' he said.

He had been right about one thing: you'd have to pry it from his cold, dead hands to take it from him; that same speech he gave to many foes who tried to steal it.

The sword was just as magnificent as the last time I'd set eyes on it, but now it was calling out to me. Of course, I had always desired it; it compelled me like human blood, consuming my senses and numbing me to all else. It looked no different than any other ordinary sword, except it did, and as it glowed with sublime aura that I had never witnessed before, I struggled to shake it off.

He can't be serious, I thought. *A weapon cannot atone for all his misdeeds, even one as powerful as this. A facile gift from a facile man – oh, how fitting.*

'You think a mere gift could absolve you of the sins of your failures?' I frowned.

'Excalibur, the most powerful sword in all of existence,' he purred, admiring the sheathed sword in his weak gasp. 'Whomsoever wields it could finish my life's work and unite the kingdoms, or bring them all to dust and the peoples of this world to their knees. It is yours alone to do with as you wish.'

'Be that as it may,' I said, disregarding the futile sentiment, 'The sword only answers to those of noble heart, and mine was defiled long ago. The sword wouldn't bend to my will and would escape my possession.'

Having said that, I would hardly consider him to be noble, I thought, *at least not in the time I have known him.*

'I had it enchanted so that only my bloodline may wield it,' he explained. 'You are its rightful heir, no matter how tainted your heart may be or however you choose to utilise it, it is yours. Surely, you most of all must know the great power of blood magic – unbreakable. Take it.'

The sword felt powerful in my grasp. Unsheathed, the blade was even more mesmerising; it entranced me. He had never let me hold his most prized possession before. In my youth, I so often dreamt of carrying it whilst aiding my father in his valiant endeavours. Now, the possibility flooded my mind.

Oh, the havoc this baby could wreak, I thought, before remembering myself. *No, I'm not worthy to wield it.*

I proceeded to rebuke my father and return his gift, not realising that the sun had already set on his life.

'He's dead!' Jeremaine whispered frantically. 'We should notify the guards before we're accused.'

'They will accuse us either way,' I eventually replied with a shrug after a brief silence, having almost forgot that Jeremaine was still in the room.

'What's your plan?' he asked.

'This sword would compel me to commit great and terrible evil,' I said. 'Despite my father's good intentions, however misguided, I cannot wield it.'

'Then what is it you intend to do?'

'We're going to return my sword back from whence it came, back into the stone, and then conceal it using the blood of its guardian. Then, no matter how tempted I may be, I won't be able to use it.'

'Who is its guardian?'

'Nimue, the Lady of the Lake.'

Brain Soup
Lucy McAllister

Confusion, the mystery of the every day
Nothing is in its proper place
Nothing is in the proper time

There is no way to make it all align
This house isn't mine.
I can't see the future
I don't have a past
I don't know what's coming and I hope this won't last
They say just in case but there is no case I can see,
that explains the confusion I can feel and see.

I'm drifting through a black hole, falling through the decades.
My memories assaulting me
My family abandoning me
They aren't what they say they are, and they say they are the impossible
The devil is at work in my mind
The pain of the confusion and tricks contort my face
The look of the lost and the lonely surrounded by loved ones with strangers' faces.

VicTory
Lucy McAllister

Bitch stole our milk we're all still sour
Number 10 rents rooms by the hour.
We are all drowning in the banks of England
Bleach the water but the coast's still not clear.
We don't like looking and pretend we can't hear
divide and flounder.

Burly lush grass and rough rolling hills,
it's just a shame we can't pay our bills.
There was no respite when they put in their notice,
austerity cuts while they drive their lotus.

We think we're so mighty like huge mountain waves.
But we're drips on their foreheads, still living in caves

We play in their fairground there's no tea in our cups,
the plebs keep on riding while bleeding from cuts
we pretend we don't notice while we mop up the blood.
We chase the sun but won't ever read it.

The economy's fucked and not in a good way
Jim didn't fix it and the rich never pay
Our lovely island is on the brink, so fuck it, let's all go
and have a big…
THINK

The Truth Is
Lucy McAlister

The truth is I am tired
Tired of the cold
Tired of the new
Tired of the old

Weary to my very core. I have no oomph anymore.
My heart is heavy and my mind is full
My body is weak and my eyes dreadful.
No amount of sleep can revive me. I am my own worst enemy.

Create and explore just to hate and deplore
Enjoy and relax but pay a heavy thinking tax
Give a queen bee some Splenda and she will die in splendour.
I just want to be at peace, a piece.

Nurture yourself and nurture your kin
You are not what you make of yourself not how you begin.
The beginning is not always the start, a life begins with learning not the beat of a heart.
The blood can run around us or out onto the streets.
The difference between death and dying is the path of the bleed.

The Juice of an Orange
Jacqueline McKenzie

There was an orange on the counter. It dropped blood-like juice, and viscus stuck to the serrated blade of the knife that lay beside it. It was mid-March, blood orange season. It didn't last so long in the UK, and you were lucky to find them. He, Peter, knew she loved them.

Her heart began to pound as beads of sweat started to appear on her brow. It was the blood, the thought of it there on the counter; blood-coloured juice splattered across the white melamine surface, dripping onto the white linoleum floor. This is where she had lost her baby three months earlier, here in the kitchen, six months pregnant. Pictures flashed before her eyes, of her leaning against the counter as the pain ripped through her insides, as the blood flooded out from between her legs, and as she sobbed and sobbed and screamed, giving birth to her tiny, dead baby girl.

She had been making a draught excluder out of leftover red satin fabric. She'd been sitting at her old Singer treadle machine in the recess space in the hall, sewing happily, and he, Peter, had been looking for a fight, one that she wasn't going to rise to as she knew where the game was going to lead. He would cause an argument out of nothing, and then use it as an excuse to go out. Not that she ever stopped him from going anywhere, but this way, there would be no questions asked; he could get up to no good and it would be her fault he had gone. She was determined that he wasn't going to pull that one on her again, but he had been tense, almost prowling along the L-shaped hallway behind her, nitpicking. She had asked him what he thought of their lovely new red satin draught excluder, and all he could reply was, 'Blood, blood, blood...it's like blood.'

'Why don't you go out and see John?' she had responded. 'You could probably do with a bit of fresh air.'

She knew he had a plan he wasn't telling her about, but she couldn't stand the tension. She knew things always went wrong he didn't get his own way. It was what her mother called wilfulness.

'Oh, you want to get rid of me, do you? OK then, I'm going,' he answered his own question, grabbing his coat and walking out of the door before she could reply.

As the door slammed behind him, she felt a sharp pain in her stomach. That was the start of it. She had called John's before things were too bad, not telling him she thought something was wrong, but he, Peter, wasn't there. A tear fell from her eye and rolled down her cheek.

He wished that on me, she thought. *It was just like he wished it on me.*

She wiped her cheek and told herself to stop being stupid. She put her bag down and grabbed a cloth from the sink, to wipe up the mess on the counter and the floor. She had always been a little paranoid, even as a child; she always needed to know her means of escape, just in case. She always noted where the drainpipes where, in case she was upstairs and needed to climb out of a window, and she would seek out the best places to hide. Deep in her subconscious, she had always held the fear that someone was coming to get her, always thinking there was a plan to kill her and that evil was lurking, waiting to get her. Was he, Peter, the evil? It was all absurd, of course. This was the 1990s after all; evil and the devil belonged in the past, or out in the deep, dark woods, and she kept on telling herself as much.

You are just paranoid, she'd think. *Nothing is going to get you. What is so important about you that would warrant such grand plots anyway?*

She had the counselling, saw the psychiatrist and put her fears down to childhood abuse, as well as her mother's preoccupation with the tarot.

'Look,' her mother had said once, 'it's like you are God and he is the devil,'

It had played on her mind, God and the devil. Was she supposed to be saving the world? Had he, Peter, come to stop her?

It had to be absurd. It was too big to comprehend, not to mention something that would get her locked up and put in a straitjacket if she dared believe it. Sometimes, though, the coincidences were frightening; the dreams that seemed to come true left her cold, and brought back fears that flashed before her like movies on a screen.

She took a plate from the cupboard, put the pieces of orange on to it and placed in the fridge. It was so much nicer cold, and she thought she would eat it later because right now she needed a cup of tea and a lie down.

Funny how something so simple as a blood orange can exhaust you emotionally, she thought.

She made the tea and went to the bedroom, sipping it along the way and wondering where he, Peter, was. She put the cup down on the table next to the bed, took off her coat and laid it over the Lloyd loom chair in the corner before slipping off her shoes and getting on the bed. She had loved this room. Before she was pregnant, she would lay on her bed in the afternoons and look out at the sky beyond the cherry tree and write: memories, imaginings, wishes, poems, and songs of every and any sort. She had been devastated when she found out he had used them all, a box full of two years' worth of soul-searching pages, to light a fire in the garden whilst she was out; the same fire he had used to burn the flowers she had planted and nurtured, and that were ready to bloom. He was apologetic enough, saying he thought the flowers were weeds and that the box of papers was just old junk that he had needed to clean up in order to clear his head. The sun stopped shining for her that day, and it snowed. It was the first time she could ever remember it snowing in June. If she hadn't just found out she was pregnant, she may have just killed herself.

She dozed off, curled up like a foetus embracing itself. In her mind, she was holding the baby she had lost. The tea went cold, and the sun had set before she woke.

The flat was silent. He, Peter, still wasn't back. She sipped on the cold tea, grabbed her dressing gown and slipped it over her clothes, then headed along the corridor past the sewing machine to the kitchen. There was silence everywhere. She didn't mind that; she didn't even mind the shadows that flickered behind her. She thought of them as friendly ghosts that would scurry out of view when she turned to capture them.

There was a knock at the door. It was his, Peter's, mother, Rosemary. That was a surprise; she didn't usually come out after five unless it was a party or special occasion.

'Hi Rosemary,' she greeted her. 'Are you OK?'

'Yes, Lindy, I'm fine,' she replied. 'Peter is worried

about you.'

'I'm fine, Rosemary. Where is he? Peter, I mean.'

'I don't know. He just rang and sounded upset – said you had caused an argument and he had gone out because you didn't want him here anymore.'

Lindy looked questioningly at Rosemary. Rosemary looked flushed and was sweating.

'Oh?' Lindy said. 'I've been out all day. I went to see a publisher about a book I want to write. When I left this morning, Peter was still in bed. We didn't argue. In fact, he was extra loving.' She reached for Rosemary's arm. 'Look, why don't you come in and sit down, you look a bit stressed. I'll give you a lift home if you like. I just need to freshen up – I've been napping. Why don't you help yourself to a drink or something while I tidy myself up?'

Rosemary agreed, going into the kitchen as Lindy went to the bathroom to brush her hair and swill her face.

What is he up to? Lindy wondered. *Why would he tell his mother lies like that?*

She looked at herself in the mirror, pondering whether she just imagined him hugging and kissing her that morning. Doubt tip-toed across her face; she squinted and moved closer to the mirror to get a good look at herself.

No, I'm sure we didn't have an argument, she reassured herself, before walking back to the kitchen where Rosemary was sitting eating the blood orange. The juice dripped over her bottom lip, and she caught it with a napkin.

'Are you sure there is nothing wrong?' she asked again.

'Yes, Rosemary, I'm sure. . .I know I've been depressed, but it's only to be expected,' she replied, looking at her stomach. 'I am picking myself up, so I don't know why he is worried. I'm sure we didn't argue this morning.'

Rosemary looked down her nose at Lindy accusingly; Lindy's face blushed red as anger started to rise and she told herself to bite her tongue. Peter would love it if she had a row with his mother, and Rosemary would love to be able to gossip about her to friends and the rest of the family, jangling about how unstable Lindy was and how terribly she had spoken to her.

'Anyway, was it good?' Lindy said, gesturing towards the orange peel on the plate and trying to sound bright and friendly. 'Peter bought it for me, even cut it up ready for me to eat when I got home.'

'Mm, it was delicious,' Rosemary replied, wiping her

hands and mouth on the napkin.

'Let's go, then,' Lindy said. 'I know you hate being out so late.'

It was 7.30, and they listened to the news on the car radio.

'I'm exhausted,' Rosemary remarked as they arrived at her home. 'It must be all the upset, rushing around to make sure you hadn't killed yourself – the worry of how I might find you.'

'Look, Rosemary, I won't deny that the thought has crossed my mind, but believe me, I am not now or ever going to kill myself. Thank you for your concern, but please don't worry about me. I can't believe he, Peter, would have concerned you like this. It was irresponsible of him.'

'Now, now, Lindy. You know he was just worried. We all know you have mental problems – he's told us all about your mood swings. It's no wonder he started drinking.'

Lindy flushed with anger as she jumped out of her seat and opened the passenger door to let Rosemary out. Her husband was standing at the door; Rosemary yawned and headed towards him as Lindy jumped back in the driver's seat and waved, shouting 'thank you,' and 'goodbye,' whilst driving off fuming.

Now, she was angry.

No, she was furious!

She had never understood the expression 'seeing red' before, but now she knew it was true that a level of anger existed that actually made everything appear red. He, Peter, was a complete and utter liar. He, fucking Peter, had probably made up lots of stories about her, with the intention of undermining her sanity.

She was driving just a little too fast, forty on a thirty road, so she put her foot on the brake to slow it down a bit when she was hit from behind by another car. The redness faded to black as she hit the steering wheel with her head.

The next night, she woke up in the hospital with her mother beside her bed.

'Where's Peter?' she asked.

'Oh, Lindy, he's with his father,' her mother answered. 'It's terrible – Rosemary's dead! They think it was an overdose.'

Lindy looked around the room, and then at the windows.

'What floor are we on, Mum?' she said, as dread pricked itself all the way from her toes to the hair follicles on her head, and the blood drained from her face.

Natural Police
David McLintock

In memory of Gopal Birdy, an L8 legend, and my friend.

Ossifer, Natural Police
Sgt Gopal strides down the corridor,
slams open the door.
Showtime Sucker!

The man/accused/wrong'un/ne'er-do-well
strikes a defiant stance but Inspector Gopal swipes
the miscreant's sweaty cheeks with a big thick
library book about planetary observations
borrowed from Windsor Street Library till
Pluto sits the guilty/probably guilty/maybe not guilty/
no, fuck it, guilty/man back on his arse.
(You've got to get promoted how you can.)

Good cop, Bad cop.
Gopal straddles the chair
like that 60's hooker brought the govt down.
He stares down the perp
(Correct this, the possibly innocent party – yawn – who cares?)
then Gopal says, Mr Kalimba's outside,
shall I bring him in and make you listen?

Writing on the Wall

The man flinches.
Or are you going to do the talking?

The possibly not guilty man manages to escape
by sky-diving out the 4th floor window.
Gopal holds his palms up –
What is it with these people?
That's four times this month.
I only open the window cos it's stuffy in here.

(Gopal says, you nicked that from Dario Fo,
didn't you? I try looking lost and innocent
but he sideswipes me with the Wetherspoons Menu Accordion
he has stuck together over many years
through unruly interviews with blood
earwax, fingernails and what have you bits of body
effluence till I confess my plagiaristic sins.)

Gopal says, do you ever drink in Chaplins?
I say, They tried to make me go to Chaplins,
I said No, No, No
(I get the Wetherspoons Treatment again)
He says, I have info you were there last week?
I say, that's cos you were giving out cake.
(I get the Wetherspoons Treatment again)
Gopal says, it was good cake wasn't it?

From the Ashes

I say, I can't remember, I got stoned.
(I get the Wetherspoons Treatment again)
And Sgt Inspector Lt Kojak, Gopal laughs.

I say, what have I done?
Gopal says, that's for me to know
and you to find out. To be honest
I haven't decided yet. Plagiarism, foraging in the park.
Being Southern is definitely up there.
I will say if you're guilty you're getting off lightly,
if you're innocent let this be a lesson to you.

He says, I like Chaplins, there are lots
of pictures of Hitler there.
I say, I think they are actually pictures of Chaplin.
He says, HAHA! So you have been there!
I've caught you in an untruth,
I've entwined you in my cunning
deceitful cop web of interrogative cunning.

Gopal says, I bought some of his artwork.
What, I say?
Hitler's. He used to live round here.
It's pretty REDACTED effing REDACTED
(Gopal advises me, I'm a PC in The Constabulary,
you plonky, not a Glowie from The Company)
but alongside my Quo collection

it's a decent nest egg.

Listen, I plead, if this gig hits the first edition…
and Gopal gets a bit Kojak sentimental
and hits me sweetly a few more times
with Mrs Wetherspoon, says,
You can't help yourself, can you?
He turns the tape to Quo collection
it's a decent nest egg.

Listen, I plead, if this gig hits the first edition…
and Gopal gets a bit Kojak sentimental
and hits me sweetly a few more times
with Mrs Wetherspoon, says,
You can't help yourself, can you?
He turns the tape to Quo
and both of us thumbs in belt-loops rock out
until the morning and my hanging.

Meech Rides Again
David McLintock

75yrs Meech marries Isabelle.
76 he gets uppity, asks May
come round. They share
fondue, it is colossal.

Is and May row
but they've been scrapping
over men their whole lives
so a couple of scratches
and it comes to nothing.

Meech gets Is a mobility doodah,
a crimson bit of kit with a flappy flag
bunted to the back. He nicked it.

She hops on, sits in his lap
they growl up the lane, back down
the rutty pavement, over the edge
of a lawn, through the heart of a pampas.

Is loves it, claps her hands and grins,
is happy to bless the pair of them
departing. Meech and May
share drips of steamy cheese,

creep all over each other,
move into a new place, bathe naked
in the back yard, arousing ire.
Meech shrugs.
Not our fault you've raised nosy kids.

A Poem For Dad
Fergus Michaelson

1) 'It's the hope that kills you.'

You picked me up
after the final whistle
after we survived
another relegation battle

you squeezed me so
I couldn't breathe
clutched my head
to your shoulder
and told me I was your good luck charm

2) 'You ungrateful little shit.'

You picked me up from the party
before I was ready
and drove me home
in silence

You were breathing angrily
so I rested my head
on the shoulder of the seat

away from you
away from the ensuing battle

We arrived home and you asked me
if I was going to thank you

I'm not sure if I ever thanked you

3) 'I'm sorry Mr Ferguson.'

I picked you up
from the wheelchair
your head collapsed
on my shoulder
the oxygen tank your breath

We watched the last day
of the season where a loss
would have condemned
us to something that
a few years prior
would have been unthinkable
and I thought about how lucky we have been.

Who is it? Who Can Tell Me Who I Am?
Mandy Morgan
(King Lear, Act 1: Scene 4)

Mal scrolled through the emails, barely glancing at the subject headings; his eyes and mind were focussed on the mangy fox currently sniffing around the bins on the path. *Clever bastards, foxes*, he thought. *I mean, where do they live?* It struck him that you never stumble across a den, despite the fact that the suburb he lived in was increasingly populated by the creatures, brazenly crossing the road in daylight, seemingly unaware that they were supposed to be nocturnal creatures and shy around humans. *Foxes and fat squirrels*. Squirrels were more of an issue, he decided. They seemed to multi-spawn every year, increasing in size and confidence, while being ignored by and large by the populace and other animals. *Shouldn't cats chase squirrels?* Next door's fat ginger seemed to render them invisible.

It was Saturday, a day traditionally filled with weekend anticipation and plans, yet there were none. Mal's fingers hovered over a 'CHEAP FLIGHTS !!!!!' email, but in a flick of a second, he ruled out any notion of escape as he leaned back and looked at the detritus pinned to the corkboard above his desk: curling newspaper articles on Julian Assange, Aaron Swartz and the Exxon Knew Campaign, plus a postcard featuring the *V for Vendetta* mask, synonymous with the Anonymous Activists, all crammed in alongside takeaway menus and a picture of his niece.

Think, he told himself. *Engage brain, think.*

The weekend – this weekend – was for introspection, self-improvement and proper plans. The desk was littered with post-it notes, each one proclaiming a question that needed to be addressed. He imagined, for a moment, having a sudden fatal heart attack and being found amongst these notes:

Where is my angry voice?!

Potential?!

How do I take control of the rest of my life?

Casual sex relationship?

Who are you?!

God, if he suffered a fatal heart attack or stroke, everyone would think he was so *sad* if they found him here amongst this procrastinating piffle (note to self, shred post-its). He picked up the 'Potential?!' – irritated by the excessive use of punctuation, absolutely no need. There was no audience, no necessity to inflect emotion; typical Mal bollocks.

Potential?!: having or showing the capacity to develop into something in the future.

His issue, the real stumbling block, was that his potential was more of the scientific kind. He'd looked it up, written it down somewhere: '...the energy possessed by a body by virtue of its position relative to others...'

He'd always needed a catalyst, and all the catalysts in his life so far had been women. What had Sonia, the slightly scary Millennial, said in the office last week? He'd joined the (male) 'chorus of disparagement and rebuff,' but actually, her theory that Macbeth would never have got his shit together without the female characters rang uncomfortably true. She had articulated, slightly nasally and with weird inflection, that, leaving the questionable morality of it all aside, without the witches and his missus, Macbeth would have never actually done anything. In a modern world, he would have watched endless YouTube videos on self-fulfilment, progression in the workplace, motivation and achieving your goals until, eventually, he possibly managed a list, but never a killing.

Rings uncomfortably true, Mal thought, looking at his post-its. *Now, focus. Back to the emails, Malcolm!*

The subject line 'We Need Your Support!!' caught his attention. He hovered the cursor over it, suspecting spam. Two rows below it was Gracie's, one of his favourite restaurants, enticing him with a discount coupon, an offering that was completely undermined by their use of Comic Sans typeface. He inwardly shuddered. *Comic Sans, along with Brush Script, should be banned*, he thought, as he started to compile a list of other offensive fonts in his head before forcibly blocking himself from going down that particular rabbit hole, recalling how his pathological dislike of certain typographic scripts had resulted in him once leaving a Chinese buffet restaurant on account of the menu being printed in Impact.

Concentrate, he told himself again. *Emails*.

'Malcolm! We Need Your Support!!' he started reading.

'Your details have been submitted to us by Ananke Hoxha. Please click the link below to confirm your identity and join our database. We recommend that you use #minefieldsecuritysolutionsuk when accessing our platform.'

Ananke? the name jumped out at him. She still had his email address? Christ, he hadn't heard from her since the Climate Camp protest in Edinburgh – what, ten years ago? More? Weird. Sitting here surrounded by his post-its, and then this.

She had been one of his catalysts, spurring him into action. Two years together, including that last summer spent at her family home in Greece, and then on to Scotland to support the demonstrations against the banks' involvement in financing environmentally damaging activities. She'd caught the eye of NJ, one of the head honchos (sanctimonious prick, further evidenced by only being known by his initials), and over the course of that week had drifted away from him in every sense, before finally announcing that she wasn't going to be leaving with him on the last day. He recalled with horrible detail the panic rising in him like bile; so sudden, so final; the selfish anger he'd felt at losing the package of her, the cheap Greek holidays, the generous allowance from her doting father and the activism adventures that she organised and managed. Oh, he had loved her – she was easy to love – but he'd leaned on her to define himself and shape his life far, far too much, to the point where perhaps she had sensed this inherent weakness within him even then; the liquid fluidity of his character, willing to adopt a shape that he had not created himself.

A quick Google cited her as the author of a paper for Public Policy Projects, specialising in climate change, environment and energy transition. Hardly surprising; her passion was proper, sincere, a forebearer of Greta Thunberg, literally around about the right age to be her mother, though Ananke wasn't the childbearing type, or least she never used to be.

Saying that, Greta's mother doesn't really look the type, either, he thought. *Wasn't she an opera singer or something?*

So, what was she doing by submitting his name to some database? He returned to the email and read it more closely. With the initial surprise having faded, the company's name, Nightjar, rang some distant bell.

Intrigued, he followed the instructions in the email, installing the recommended security software before accessing the platform. *What the hell is she up to?* he asked himself, not finding much on the initial page. 'An activist group specialising in nonviolent direct action...' *ah, here it is*. '..seeking to recruit like-minded computer specialists for a forthcoming project working with...'

Below the text was just a symbol, a sort of infinity figure of eight in a circle, and then a further link.

So, she's assumed that I'd still be working in the computer science field, he thought, not knowing whether to be flattered that she still thought of him enough to take the trouble to send the link, or disappointed that she had presumed he would still be in the same work and on the same email address.

He scrolled down further, scanning for more information. What was the gig? They clearly wanted tech-savvy mischief-makers to target someone or something significant. He returned to the infinity eight symbol, copied it and slapped it into the search engine.

Nothing. Literally nothing.

He found himself looking at a host of symbols, but none of them had the distinctive number eight in the centre. Inwardly sighing, he minimised the page and clicked on the Tor icon. He was trying to wean himself off the dark web and had in fact only reinstalled the Tor search engine a week before, after months of abstinence. Not that he got up to anything too dodgy; he just felt safer being protected by anonymity while he browsed.

Mal's phone vibrated twice, a signal that a message had arrived. Leaving the search bar empty, he glanced at his phone: Message from Maddy. He'd been hoping that she would get in touch about meeting up, but now he was intrigued by the email and wanted to do a deep dive and find out more.

'Meet me, have NEWS!!!'

This could only mean one thing with Maddy; there would be a man story that she was desperate to share. He gave a soft snort, knowing there was no need to reply. His instructions would swiftly follow.

'11.30 Donovan's, table at the back :)'

It had already gone 10.30, and Donavan's was a good fifteen minutes' walk away.

Infinity Eight would have to wait.

Maddy's effervescence was contagious, and the lunch had been long, entertaining and lager-soaked. She'd arrived, predictably late, in an out-of-season floppy hat and huge shades; denying it was any form of disguise, she'd promptly discarded the hat, but managed to maintain the glasses for a good twenty minutes before balancing them precariously on her head and holding court on her latest date/scam/ disaster/adventure.

Mal revelled vicariously in Maddy's tales. They had worked together on a couple of projects before she went freelance, and he missed her energy and enthusiasm, not to mention her constant ribbing of him. He'd thought about sharing the email with her, but something made him want to keep it to himself for now. Maddy would trample all over it in her Doc Martens, as for all her exuberant flamboyance, she was surprisingly conformist when it came to rules. Not that he was much of a radical these days, the odd online petition aside. He couldn't remember the last time he'd actively pursued a cause, hence the 'Where's my angry voice?' Post-it note. He missed it; activism had always made him feel somehow more alive and energised, part of something. It would be good to get his teeth into something.

I am going to take this further, then? he thought.

Back at home, he felt the beginnings of a post-lager headache starting – fight it with a coffee or continue drinking? The temptation to do the latter was great, but then the day would be lost and he had been determined to achieve some goals over the weekend. Whilst the coffee brewed, he thought about Nightjar and Infinity Eight, considering his possible involvement. He knew he had the skills they would be after; working in the Security Operations Centre of an international telecommunications company for the previous five years had furnished him with a plethora of expertise in threat hunting and investigation. He had supplemented this experience with a StaxR ethical hacking course, and whilst not a Certified Ethical Hacker, he had acquired the knowledge necessary to be a 'White Hat.' So, assuming these groups had nefarious intent, could he – would he – make the switch and become a 'Black Hat' hacker?

At his desk, he gathered the post-its up, wondering how many of them would be addressed if he went down this path. *Too easy*, he brought himself up sharply. *This flight of fancy will get me nowhere.* He was yet again jumping on someone else's bandwagon without any sense of personal commitment (or knowledge) of their cause, ironically using Ananke as his facilitator again after all these years, blindly projecting himself into the dark side from a position of complete ignorance.

First thing's first, investigate Nightjar and Infinity Eight.

Even on the dark web, there was a scarcity of results on Nightjar. What he did find out was that it was founded in 2013 and characterised by anti cyber surveillance and censorship acts, targeting governments, organisations and corporations.

OK, so like Anonymous, he thought, *but no hivemind.*

These guys seemed to have a clear leadership structure (no names), and were so far under the radar that they didn't feature in a standard internet search; no self-publicity, no laying claims to their seemingly unreported acts of disruption; operating furtively, apparently known to exist to only a chosen few, or maybe Nightjar were supplying hacks to other organisations or projects, which could explain Infinity Eight. He wondered why the name seemed vaguely familiar if they were this clandestine. *Linked to Ananke...of course! The heinous NJ!*

Although he knew that those initials stood for Nigel Jones, Nightjar was a far classier backronym.

He leaned back and sighed.

No denying the catalyst; all roads led back to Ananke.

Hero
Sarah Murray

Travis

It's an easy trap to fall into, thinking you're insignificant, that nothing you do really makes a difference. We spend so much of our lives trying to do something meaningful, to be remembered after we die, and yet it's often the mundane things that can make the biggest impact. As sad as it may seem to admin, the most profound thing I ever did was die. My accidental death has directly benefitted the world a million times more than anything I tried to do when I was alive. One moment of inattention caused so much darkness, but with it came so much light.

Let me tell you my story.

My name is Travis. At the time of my death, I was a twenty-eight-year-old IT consultant, engaged to my fiancé Greta. Greta was a year older than me and a decade wiser; she was a primary school teacher, and was so sweet and patient, she put Miss Honey to shame. We were in Nerja, on the Costa del Sol, scouting wedding venues. I can still remember the first time I saw her; it wasn't one of those 'our eyes met across the room' romantic meetings. She had come into my workplace to get help with her laptop; she was nearing the end of her Master's thesis and it had crashed, so she'd come in panicking because it wouldn't come back on. As I dismantled her laptop and copied over the contents of her hard drive, she blurted out all of the stresses she was under: the useless boyfriend she'd finally ditched, the high expectations of her parents due to being the first in her family to go to university, and the amount of debt she had got into during four years of studying as a mature student. I listened and made empathetic noises, all the while inwardly jumping for joy upon hearing she was single. When I managed to rescue her thesis, she threw her arms around my neck and said I was her hero. I said if that was true then she owed me a drink, and she smiled. She stayed at mine that night and never really left. We made it official two months later when she moved in, and we were happy for five years before I popped the question on a last-minute cheap package holiday in Malaga. We discussed what kind of wedding we wanted (it would have to be a Spanish wedding, surely. We'd got engaged there after all), how many kids we wanted (three: two girls, Elise and Melody; one boy, Milo), where we wanted to live (the Cheshire suburbs in a four-bed house, so the kids could each have their own room, with a big back yard and a big, bouncy doodle dog). We had everything planned and our whole lives ahead of us; it was all going to be so amazing. I can still see her now, asleep in the passenger seat, not a care in the world.

Mateo

We received the call of a major incident late on a Thursday evening. As the truck climbed the mountain, it became clear that this was a bad one; the smoke could be seen from miles away. When we arrived, there were already four other fire trucks on the scene, along with seemingly every ambulance in Malaga. We spoke with the chief of one of the other trucks, who said they were managing to evacuate those on the bus who had survived the crash, but that the car was further down the mountainside and difficult to access. They were unsure if there would be any survivors inside.

I volunteered to climb down and make an assessment; the climb was treacherous, and I slipped more than once. I nearly turned back, but the thought of someone being alone and injured on the mountainside spurred me on. When I got over the bluff and saw the car, it was difficult to see how anyone could have survived, and then I saw them. She was kneeling over him, administering CPR. I called out and she looked up, waving at me to come help. I scrambled over to her, and she began to explain something in English. My English was pretty broken, as was her Spanish, but I managed to figure out that she had been performing CPR since the crash happened, nearly two hours before. I radioed back for helicopter assistance and took over CPR; it was clear that the man was dead, but she was so desperate and had fought so heroically, I couldn't bring myself to give up. She was injured and exhausted, but when the helicopter landed, she was insistent that the man be loaded before her, and that CPR be continued the whole way to the hospital. I caught up with her again later, after she had come out of surgery with a pin in her broken leg. She had just been informed of the man's death – her fiancé, as it turned out – and was inconsolable. She had no family of friends in the country, so I offered to stay with her. I didn't want her to be alone on such a sad day. Her fiancé was already being blamed for the crash – the survivors reported him as driving on the wrong side of the road – and some of the families of the bus victims were at the hospital, looking for someone to blame. She cried herself to sleep that night, not for the last time either. Even years later, long after we married, I would sometimes find her silently crying herself to sleep. It would be some significant date – his birthday, their anniversary or the day he proposed to her – as even with all of the love she had for both me and our daughter, she still mourned him to her last day.

Greta
I didn't even notice the missed period at first; too much of my usual routine had changed for the alarm bells to start ringing. I noticed the second missed period,

though, and, stupidly, for a moment, I wondered if it was Travis'. It seemed daft now; he'd been dead six months by that point, and I'd had innumerable blood tests, x-rays, and scans in the months immediately following the crash, all of which would've shown up a baby pretty quickly. Not to mention, I'd have a pretty sizeable bump by six months! But still, for one, beautiful moment, I thought I might still have a piece of him with me. Then came the realisation that if Travis wasn't the father, it could only be one other person: Mateo, the fireman who rescued us from the mountainside. That one stupid mistake I made six weeks before while drunk and hurting after the inquest ruled Travis culpable for the deaths of those poor nineteen people on the bus...Jesus Christ, how was I going to explain this to people? How could I look his parents in the eye and tell them I was pregnant by a man who was practically a stranger, when my fiancé's body was barely cold in the ground? Plus, he lived in Spain, so how the hell was that going to work?

Life, however, has a way of making things work. Mateo was an absolute hero; he said he would do whatever I wanted: be involved, not be involved, but still send money to support the baby; support me if I wanted an abortion. He really was amazing about the whole thing, and so as much as I hadn't wanted a baby – definitely not with some random Spanish man – when

I saw the ultrasound, I knew I was going to keep it. Mateo offered to move to the UK to allow me to stay by my family, but their judgemental attitude and the whispers from people in the street became too much for me and so, at four-and-a-half months pregnant, I decided to move over to Spain, at least for a short time. There were difficulties with affording the healthcare over there, though, and so it was decided, for practical reasons, that Mateo and I should get married in order for me to access the healthcare system for free as his spouse. Our wedding day was quiet, attended by just his family and a handful of friends, and conducted simultaneously in Spanish and English. Afterwards, we went to a restaurant for a meal. I was seven months pregnant at the time, meaning that while everyone else celebrated, I turned in to bed early and cried myself to sleep.

Before I knew it, the joyful day came. I went into labour at 2:30am on the morning of 27th May, and Sofia was with us by seven. The rush of love was like nothing I'd ever felt before, and it gave me the strength to resolve that I would buck my ideas up and start smiling again. I may not have chosen this life, but through a weird series of unexpected events, I had found myself holding the most perfect and precious angel I had ever seen.

For her sake, I had to move on.

Sofia

Today, I gave an interview about my research, and found myself talking about my mother. It got me thinking about everything she went through in her life: the crash, losing her fiancé, the cancer...I remember, when I was eight, her telling me that she was poorly and would have to take some medicine that might make her hair fall out. She bought lots of brightly coloured wigs and, when she was well enough, we would take it in turns to try them on and invent characters. There was Svetlana the Russian spy, Daisy the milkmaid, and Old Mother Jones; we'd give them backstories and act out plays for my father when he came home from work. When the cancer returned, I was twelve, and once again, out came the wigs. This time, I would help her draw her eyebrows back on and add some blush, while the chemo drained away her strength and colour. She never complained, never lamented her lot in life. Whenever people would ask about her bad luck, she would simply say that everything in her life had brought her to my father and me, so how could anything be so bad if it led to such happiness? I'm sure she must have had her down moments where she cried or got angry, but I don't remember them. When she beat it for the second time, we took a family trip to New York to celebrate. That was an amazing holiday, and Mama had the time of her life.

There were no wigs when the cancer returned for the third and final time. It had been hiding, lurking in the background, spreading. This time, there would be no chemo; at most, it would have bought her maybe a few months. Mama decided that she wanted to be as healthy as possible in the time she had left, so we set about making enough memories to last a lifetime. As she got weaker, my father would carry her to bed or to the bathroom, and she would thank him for rescuing her once more. He would thank her for rescuing him from a life of loneliness. I suppose it's no surprise, then, that I went into oncology research, dedicating twenty years of my life to killing the thing that took my mother from me. I finally did it too: 95% remission rate, and we're pushing for the full 100%. I know she would be so proud.

When I arrive home from the lab, I left myself into the house and hear laughter from the other room; my father is entertaining my girls with stories of his firefighting days – embellished, of course – and acting out the stories just like we did for him all those years ago. After putting the girls to bed, he and I go into the garden to perform the old familiar ritual; the single candle of my childhood has doubled with my mother's passing, as we give thanks to Travis, the man who brought us all together, and to the woman who made us both heroes. – Just like her.

Mermaid's Tale
Hana Musimurimwa

I hold my breath and jump. My heart beats so fast with excitement, but my head is panicking. Are you going to follow my lead?

I can't stop going over all the words you said yesterday. Are you thinking about our conversation too? Was it as important to you, as it was to me?

I am hoping, but sometimes I feel like I am not coping anymore – just playing along. Aren't we all? Are we all on this journey of growing strong only to keep failing and breaking, ignoring all the mistakes we are making? Is everybody living life like this, with all the ups and downs? I have no idea.

Please, hold your breath and jump after me! We can swim in this life together and do better. Not looking back – just always having each other's back. Hurry up! I am waiting.

Sometimes I hate to feel that small when from the outside it might look like I have it all. But who cares what other people think, right? Their idea of me is changing with a blink and I am still the same. Living in my bubble. Or is it our bubble?

I have to swim to the surface. I need a breath of fresh air. So, am I gonna do it now or can I last a bit longer? Are you ready to jump? Should I wait? Maybe I should just become a mermaid.

Mother
Hana Musimurimwa

Her love was made for eternity, mother.

The beauty of the world that is burning and almost forgetting. Mother
All the words of encouragement followed by guilt but never regretting. Mother

Your tears, your body, your heart so warm and giving. Mother
I am running with no fear of falling apart, just like you. Mother

I have the invisible shield to win the fight, you can do it. Mother
Giving me the ticket for the flight and always waiting. Mother

The journey or education and growing wiser. Mother
New heartbeat, unconditional fear and love, dedication. Mother

Hana, the lucky one, that's who you became. Mother
So never forget your worth, your name. Mother.

Riot

Hana Musimurimwa

I am sure of uncertainty
knowing all about not knowing.
I believe in relativity,
So where are we all going?

Running so fast,
always overtaking, racing
How long are we going to last
and fight the monsters we are facing?

Can we stop the world spinning
and let the present moment be our treasure?
How do we decide who is losing or winning?
How does this measure?

Stop!

Love, appreciation, unity and only one nation.
With all that gained head immunity
Who needs more soul isolation?
Are we ready for a munity?

Turn around, throw the crown,
Do you see the future repeating?

Writing on the Wall

Trying to push you down
And constantly mistreating.

What is the point of knowing
when we keep failing to remember?
The vessels of power are still rowing
How do I become a member?

What is the point of believing
when we keep lying?
The treaties are being signed
But people are still dying.

Get up and stop crying!

Those who can't speak up need us to be loud, our voices to shout
And never be quiet.
We are sure of the riot!

Never Forgotten
Hana Musimurimwa

A face full of wrinkles and a heart full of life, that is Bob. This 90-year-old gentleman lives in a care home, and he feels really special these days – a real book is being written about his life. Even though he wouldn't count these past two years as living, he feels peace when he closes his eyes. He had an amazing life full of ups and downs, but that is the exciting stuff. If you know how to live you also know how to die.

Will everyone know his story now? Does this mean he will be famous even when he's not here? Oh definitely! His friends will be so jealous, and all the old ladies with their pointy glasses up on the third floor will read the book and wish they'd made more of a fuss of him while his heart was still beating. They do adore him though, everyone in the home does. His family loves him too, but this bloody pandemic, full of coughs and closed doors and people pushed so far from each other. Their letters keep him connected. These weekly reminders of belonging somewhere are the food for his soul.

The journalist, Jo, visits him weekly. She is young, fit and knows how to make him feel important. He loves to joke with her and flirt a little. It's pretty amusing to watch how funny she finds it, although she sometimes looks a little uncomfortable too.

'Hello Jo, my darling, I've missed you,' he says when she appears in the doorway. 'Let me have a better look at you.' He's holding a bed remote control and glides into a more seated position. 'Very, very nice. As always!'

Jo giggles, oh boy, here we go again. 'Hello, you, nice to see you again. So, what's new? How have you been?'

'Are you really asking me what's new? Do you realise where I am living these days?!' he cries with a laugh that turns into a heavy cough. Then he smiles. 'Should we start with the book stuff, my love?'

'I'd be happy to. Last time you told me about your work and the war and you started telling me about your family. We covered your wedding, marriage, your daughter and I believe that you have only one granddaughter?' Jo was holding her pen and nervously tapping the paper with it.

'If you weren't writing that book, I'd say you're being incredibly nosy,' said Bob. 'And yes, this little bundle of joy was brought into our lives and changed my life forever. Mischievous little thing. You see, I always enjoyed being a dad, but was so busy working, that I never really got to enjoy it the way I wanted to. With my granddaughter it was different because I retired when she was born. I had all this time on my hands and Anne was always holding one of them. Being gramps was the best role I've ever had, and I must admit, I was pretty good at it. You should ask my granddaughter yourself one day.' He winked at Jo who was writing down every word he'd said.

'When she was a baby, she used my beer belly as a pillow to have these perfect naps.' He laughed and coughed at the same time. 'When she was a bit older, we'd go on adventures to a nearby forest almost every day. Backpacks full of snacks and days full of exploring the woods, the valleys and ponds. Picnics in summer and ice skating in winter.'

His eyes were bright like the eyes of a little boy as his mind carried him back. 'I could play with these blond plastic dolls for hours or tell her stories about wooden toys that come to life. She loved it. She told me many times that I was her best friend.' He lifted his chin with pride like he'd just received the Nobel prize for being a best friend to this young lady. 'There is nothing more genuine than hearing this from a kid, they really mean these things, you know?'

Bob's face came back from his dream, and he leaned forward, looking straight into Jo's eyes. She got goosebumps. 'Do you have a nice relationship with your grandpa, Jo? Stop writing your notes for a minute and tell me something about yourself too!' he cried. Jo jumped at the sound of her name.

'Oh yes, of course ... ehm ...'

Bob wiggled impatiently. 'Oh, come on, you are like what, 30 years old? Married? Any kids?' He showered her with questions.

Jo's face was still. 'Yes, you are right. I am 32 and I am married, indeed. I have a three-year-old little girl, Lily. You might see her later if you wish, my husband is picking me up today.'

Bob's face lit up. He couldn't really move, but his mind jumped with excitement. 'Yes! I would love that! Does she take after her mum? Is she as curious as you?'

Jo smiled. 'She definitely has my manners and my character. She's a cheeky little thing,' she added. Bob laughed. Jo continued, 'To get back to your question, my grandpa used to be my best friend too. An absolute gem of a guy – funny, sharp and he always had an answer for everything. We had so much fun together when I was little.'

Bob nodded. 'He sounds like my kind of person. How is he doing these days? Is he still handsome like me or has the age thing got him?' He turned his head to the side, winked and clicked his tongue. Jo giggled and rolled her eyes. 'He is very much still a gaffer.' They smiled at each other.

'It sounds to me like he might be the reason you write these books about old people. Out of respect? Or do you just have a thing for older gentlemen like me in general?' He wanted to laugh but started coughing instead and couldn't catch his breath.

'Are you OK?' Jo stood up. 'Would you like some water? Should I call the nurse?'

'Oh no, I'm fine. Where is that little girl of yours, is she coming? How do I look? Wouldn't want to scare the tiny princess off.' He started fidgeting.

'You look great as always Bob. Let me check my messages.' She dug her phone out of her handbag and put her notes and pen back inside. 'Yes, they are already here, waiting in the car. Would you like my husband to bring her upstairs to meet you?'

'One hundred percent, tell them to hurry up!'

'Bob, tell me, before she comes, where is your granddaughter now? Do you keep in touch?' Jo asked shyly.

'She's doing great. Living her best life. She writes me letters – she is a mother now too, so her little one keeps her busy. You know what I'm talking about. I am sure they are going to visit me soon, but until then I must be happy with the letters. I love her dearly …'

Before he could finish the sentence, a little girl burst into the room. 'Mummy! Mummy! Mummy! Daddy got me a new toy! Look! Look!'

'Lily, this is Bob.' Jo told her.

'Hello! Hi! Look at my new doll! Look!' Lily was unstoppable.

Bob beamed down at the little girl. 'Hello Lily, so

lovely to meet you. What an amazing dolly you have there.' Time passed, nursery rhymes were sung and hearts were melted. 'I am a bit tired now, Jo. Will you come next week again to crack on with the book?'

Lily ran back to the hallway to show her toy to the nurses. Jo held Bob's hand. 'Of course. We are getting your story out there. This amazing life will never be forgotten.'

Bob was as proud as a peacock. 'Looking forward to it. Your little girl reminds me of my granddaughter. Anne had the same blazing eyes. You know, her name is actually Joanne, but she wanted everyone to call her Anne. Very stubborn lady.'

Jo smiled. 'I bet she can't wait to see you again. She must love you very much.'

Bob was already dozing off as Jo took all her things and left the room. She picked up her phone and dialled her mum's number.

'Hi dear, so how was he today? Has he remembered anything?'

'He wanted to see Lily. You should come with me next week and I can introduce you as my editor if you'd like.'

'I don't know about that Anne. I mean, I don't know how you do it, seriously. I would just burst into tears; it breaks my heart.'

Joanne said goodbye to her mum and walked swiftly to the car. Her family was waiting. Her heart was full. He doesn't remember, but she will never forget.

See you next week, my best friend.

Waiting for the 82
Rachel Naomi

A pregnant lady was lingering at the bus stop outside the bombed-out church. She often thought of painting, although she made empanadas and sweet black coffee for a living. Her eyes and hair were the shade of a raven's feather; she had enough height, standing in a grey sweater dress which hovered below the calf. It stuck to her body, dabbing it in sweat stains that gave it the appearance of a Rorschach test.

Her calloused heels first stepped on the city's concrete pavements in May. Anyone's arrival to any city is eventful for a time, until even the person arriving forgets they were once unfamiliar with a place. By the time July snuck around, it was hot – hot for an English summer, anyway. Regardless, she carried around a scarf that her mother gave her, one that resembled a keffiyeh, though her mom never discussed its origins. She brought the scarf with her in case there were accidents, or if she got cold, as she often found herself, though on occasion she might have pretended it was the temperature.

She waited, as she always did on the second Monday of the month, for the bus to take her home. The pregnant lady kept to herself, out of habit. She made a point to come into the city centre once a month to discuss her brother, who had died twelve years prior. It seemed like an odd place to remember a dead brother, but this city was as good as anywhere else, especially if the cry of a seagull in the morning came and brought her to tears.

At the meeting, she spoke briefly with two sisters, both of whom had also lost brothers. The woman's own brother had used a gun, and had died of undiagnosed sadness. She was in awe of how the sisters could choose proper sneakers for themselves, ones that had minty accents and bubble gum pink flares; how they wore eyeshadow that sparkled. The pregnant lady wore canvas *alpargatas* with the city's flotsam and jetsam of cigarette ash and used receipts attached to their soles.

It was well past nine in the evening when she got to the bus stop. She was not a fastidious timekeeper, but with no bus for forty minutes, she asked someone if one was on the way. Her *tía* taught her to always ask three people any street question to be sure of its accuracy. Truth is, a woman on her own is a revolutionary act, especially if it's a woman moving through a city on her own.

That's most countries when we really get down to the nitty gritty, isn't it?

There were four people at the bus stop: a couple and two men. One man had superglued his mobile phone to his fingertips, the other was shoving loose lined paper into a leather satchel, and the couple were squatting on the church steps, their legs intertwined so tightly that it was nearly impossible to see whose jeans belonged to whom.

The pregnant lady approached the couple slowly. The young woman with a septum piercing, lemon-lime hair and a Liverpool University purple lanyard dangling upside down from her neck told her that the bus should have been by now. Then, the young man said he wasn't sure of the timetable, but that the drivers sometimes go on strike. After a few minutes, the stranger with bright hair had told her about her impossibly difficult mathematics course, her fears of dropping out and her wish to start a girl band instead. The pregnant woman asked if the land of this city had memories, and there was a pause before she answered, 'I guess so,' before going back to maths. Eventually, the boy started to talk, explaining that he wanted to start a record company. When they became bored of the chat, they told the woman they had to be on their way and headed towards the neon lights and bars with dirty floors. The young woman's hair flickered against the white LED strip lights of a nearby takeaway selling greasy kebabs, while her lover's brown ringlets bounced ever so slightly beneath his charcoal beanie.

More people arrived at the stop. The man with the

phone paced awkwardly. He asked the pregnant woman if the bus was coming, peeked at his phone again. She answered that she couldn't be sure as he scanned his phone again. He walked away, glancing at his phone and chucking his maroon coffee cup into a trash can.

Dusk became dark. Across the street, a college student in a daffodil-yellow track suit was approached by three young boys on a bike. They asked her if it hurt when she fell from the sky, and when that didn't work, the tallest one told her that she reminded him of the sun and he'd need to wear sunglasses around her, and at this she cackled loudly, so that it echoed down the alley she had half-sprinted through. The youngest boy asked for her TikTok handle; she flipped the bird at all three. They shrugged and went to try their hand at buying a few cans of anything. The pregnant woman watched the young woman walk away, and then looked down at her feet, which she couldn't see because of her protruding belly. She thought to herself that her young daughter, back at home, must be sleeping soundly in her bed by now.

A thin elderly man moved with urgency, shoved his papers into his leather satchel and now was removing each one, reading it quickly, folding it, and then returning it. He had been waiting as long as she had. She asked him if the buses were running this late. He told her that buses never arrive on time in this country. She thought about the buses in the other places she had been; she was amazed that people felt safe enough to pull out their phones on the street here. Some of her friends would still have mini heart attacks when even a dog passed them. He asked her about her accent, and she told him about it as he kept folding his papers. They waited. He told her about his time in Spain, a place she'd never been to. Her only connection being her surnames found upon a lengthy list of expelled Sephardim people. Still the buses did not pass. In one whole sentence, he told her about a business he once had in Toledo and how he could speak *un poquito*...but just *un poquito*.

His business went under after Brexit.

His eyes were the colour of a river, though she couldn't remember which one. He paused, looked at the pregnant lady, then noticed a bus out of the corner of his eye. The Pastaza river, that was the colour she remembered. He waved frantically, but the bus didn't stop.

'And sometimes, they go right past yiz,' he said, and then shuffled off down the street.

Her son kicked her insides like he was tubing down the Napo River. People were always asking how many weeks she was. 'A lot of weeks,' she'd answer. Keeping track of numbers exhausted her. She did things from the land; a woman at the group told her to speed up the process by walking around John Lewis' for a while, eating a spicy curry and having lots of sex.

The pregnant lady waited. More people arrived, waited and looked at their watches. Some snacked on Liquorice All-Sorts, or sipped from fizzy Vimto cans, and two men jaywalked across the street without looking up from their polystyrene boxes of fried chicken and salt-and-pepper French fries. When they reached the bus stop, they asked the pregnant lady if the buses were running. She told them she wasn't sure; they waited for a while, stinking up the air with burnt chicken skin and then biting off the last bits of meat from their drumsticks and heading down the street to the next stop. The pregnant lady was not hungry (though people think that pregnant women are *always* hungry). In fact, her stomach churned often.

'I feel bad for you, love,' a raspy voice spat, in between chunks of crunchy crisp chewing. She noticed a man lounging on the steps of the church a few feet away. 'Youz being pregnant 'n all dat.'

She explained to him that he should be happy for her.

'I don't know how youz women do it.' He paused to wipe his hands on his windbreaker. 'You rich?' he asked, before answering himself. 'Eh, must not be if yer waiting for the bus like us.' She smiled. He smiled. He introduced himself and told her about his own children. 'The buses ain't coming, love.'

The pregnant lady looked around. A few people were still waiting at the stop, many of them scrolling their phones for a possible update. She walked to the glass crate that passed for some sort of bus shelter and looked at the printed schedule again. Indelible pen ink of teenage love was scrawled over the cracked plastic housing the times.

'Best bet is for ya to walkadown thattaways.'

He pointed in the direction where the two men with fried chicken had gone.

There were some blinking signs in the distance, but she wasn't sure of anything up ahead. He flashed her a smile and dipped his fingers once more into a Tesco bag, where he had shoved another teracycle bag of smoky bacon crisps. He licked crumbs from each fingertip, his tongue covered in a thrush of artificial flavouring.

The night smelled of wafting blackcurrant vape smoke; there wasn't much noise from the traffic. Tottering up Bold Street was an inebriated man who belted out, 'love to take a walk down the Anfield Road, me and me old pal Joe-e-e-e-e,' as he stumbled forward, bumping his shoulder into brick. 'We love to see the lasses with their red scar-r-r-fs on, we love to hear the Kopites roar-r-r!'

He swung his drink around, stumbling into the road momentarily before a hackney cab slammed his palm to the horn. She thought how simple it would be to step out in front of one of the souped-up cars, or all those buses passing by on detours. Then, she thought she could just as easily walk home.

'Love, don't you worry,' the crisp-fingered man said before walking off.

Her husband was waiting for her; her daughter should be asleep. She figured she could walk from the city centre. The weather was humid, but not suffocating, like the darkness had finally allowed the air to take a breath and be itself.

A woman with hair the colour of papaya approached the stop. She waited. The blue light of her phone shone, gave glimpses of her freckles. She couldn't have been but two years younger, or two years older, than the pregnant lady. The women did not speak. The pregnant lady kept staring at the young woman's dungarees, amazed that she could pull off such a look. She wondered what it would be like to not be pregnant, and to be getting off work at this hour. Then, the overall-wearing woman said, 'You know the big Tesco? I live right past there. You wanna split a taxi?'

She told the pregnant women about her job at a coffee shop, how her co-workers were catty and that she really wanted to be an actress. She trained to become an actress, but tired of it. The pregnant woman listened. She felt the baby kicking. She pulled out a few pound coins and split the fare.

As she walked through the door, her husband handed her a glass of pineapple juice while giggling. She looked at herself in the mirror, at her smudged eyeliner and her feet covered in soot. The pregnant lady took a scolding bath until her skin turned the colour of achiote paste. She listened to *Petite Suite, En bateau* by Debussy, and when the day was switching into the next, she told her husband it was time to get to the Women's Hospital.

Her son had decided that this day was as good a day as any to be born.

The English Way
C.D. Phillip

Fade in – Int. Box Bedroom – Day
Julie (19) *sits on her bed surrounded by unpacked boxes. The detritus of a younger girl's weekly stays surrounds her. Off screen – door slam.*

Julie: You said you hadn't touched anything…I wasn't expecting…

Julie gestures to everything. **Aaron (50)** – *a plainly dressed man with a regional accent flattened for office 'professionalism' – enters, carrying more boxes.*

Aaron: Your room equals your mess, love. I just closed the door. *(He places the boxes down and stretches)* Finished. Have you considered becoming one of those lesbians that doesn't wear makeup?
Julie: What now that we've got all the boxes upstairs? You offered to help Dad, me and Rin could have handled it.
Aaron: Ah, it got done quicker us all doing our share. I'm putting the kettle on. Do you want one? And Rin?
Julie: They had to take the truck back. I'll take one though.
Aaron: Sure thing, you keep on.

Julie: Thanks, Dad.

Aaron exits. Julie makes the motions of unpacking. Aaron returns hovering in the doorway.

Aaron: So…Rin. Are you and her –
Julie: They
Aaron: What?

Julie looks up worried about his reaction but it's important to her that he respects her friend.

Julie: They use they/them pronouns.
Aaron: Oh. I didn't – How do you know when people are…thems?
Julie: Well, Dad, you trek up the gender mountains to the mystic spring. Or you can just ask them.
Aaron: Alright! Less of the sass, it's not too late for you to be sleeping on the balcony.
Julie: What were you asking about me and Rin?
Aaron: I just wondered if you two were…
Julie: Dad you're the only one who didn't turn on me, if I was dating anyone, I would just introduce them to you.
Aaron: They didn't turn on you, love.
Julie: Didn't they? It feels like it.
Aaron: Mum loves you. She's just worried about your

safety. It's all parents ever worry about.

Flashback begins. Int – 70s Master Bedroom – Night.
Mother (30s) – *feathery shag hairstyle deflating – smiles from the dressing table where she puts on her makeup.* **Aaron (child)** *watches enraptured as she paints her eyelids blue. He reaches out with greedy child fingers for her lipstick. She slaps his wrist.*

Mother: You know better. *(She taps her knee. He scrambles up eagerly)* You're getting too old for this, lad. *(She smiles sadly, brushing her fingers through his hair)* Not a word to your dad.

Aaron nods, closing his eyes as she pats his face with the makeup brushes, before tapping the lipstick onto his bottom lip. He pops his lips exaggeratedly, opening his eyes and beaming.

Aaron: I'm beautiful!
Mother: *(She chuckles)* Now wipe it off, I want you changed for bed before we leave.

Aaron beams at his reflection.

Int – Secondary School Bathroom – Day
Aaron (15) – *Stares into a grimy school bathroom mirror.*

He's taken a beating. Blood oozes from his split lip. **Tom (15)** *– a slighter boy – hovers. He tries to dab at Aaron's face with a wad of wet tissue but Aaron shoves him away.*

Aaron: Get away from me.
Tom: Sorry. Sorry.
Aaron: You should be! It's your fault.
Tom: I think *they're* to blame –
Aaron: But who set them off? If you just –
Tom: Just what?
Aaron: I don't know! Were normal maybe? Then I wouldn't have to –
Tom: Have to?! I don't remember asking you to –
Aaron: You don't have to cause I – cause we're mates…
Tom: I thought we were.
Aaron: Well it would be easier if you didn't act like such a –
Tom: Such a what?
Aaron: You know…

Tom stares at him before leaving without a word. Aaron glares at his reflection. Smearing the blood across his lips with the back of his hand.
Int – Terrace Hallway – Day
Aaron (15) *comes through the front door clutching a shopping bag.*

Mother: *(offscreen)* Is that you Aaron?
Aaron: Yeah, sorry…bus was late.

Aaron tries to drop the bag surreptitiously as Mother enters, herding in **Barbara (13).**

Mother: You're just in time, your dad hasn't left yet
Barbara: What's this?

Barbara grabs the bag before Aaron can stop her.

Aaron: Give it back

Barbara pulls out a ruffly shirt and bursts out laughing.

Barbara: Oh, I am sorry *Adam Ant*.
Aaron: Piss off
Mother: Language!

Silence falls. On the landing **Father (40s)** *looms over the family. Aaron grabs his shirt and stuffs it away.*

Barbara: Aaron brought a dress!

Father walks downstairs each step echoing.

Aaron: No…no I didn't. I just –

Father cuts Aaron off with a look and holds out his hand. Aaron hands the bag over. Father crushes it in his fist but says nothing, he turns to Mother.

Father: I'm off, love. *(He bumps a kiss on his wife's cheek)* Love you, princess. *(He does the same with Barbara. He turns to Aaron, his posture tight)* Take care of them while I'm gone.
Aaron: Of course, Dad.
Father: *(Father nods and heads to the door with Aaron's bag)* I'll get ride of these.
Aaron: What? Dad no!
Father: *(Turns around)* What was that?
Mother: *(Steps between them. She brushes Father's collar down)* It's getting late, dear.

Father looks down at her, giving a tight smile. He exits. Mother sighs and untenses.

Aaron: Mum –
Mother: It's for your own good Aaron…Come on, I'll put the kettle on.

Int – Bedroom – Day
Julie and Aaron sit on the bed between the boxes holding their mugs of tea.

Julie: Do you really think she'll come around?
Aaron: I can't promise you…but I do, yes.
Julie: What made you accept me?
Aaron: *(stares into his tea)* I didn't want you to waste your life, to wake up one day miserable and realise it's too late. *(he looks up, his eyes wet)* I want you to be happy, love.

Julie hugs Aaron.

Julie: *(whispers)* Maybe…maybe we could both be happy?

Aaron pulls away.

Aaron: Nah, love. I'll leave happiness to the young.

Fade out.

Scousers Coven
Amanda Pinnington

Ya know when someone gives you too much information, too quickly and your brain dies, and you can't understand what they're saying? And everyone's screaming, shouting, and panicking all around you and you just wanna tell them all to fuck off? Well, that's how it was, and I just needed a minute.

'Everyone shut up' I shouted, and they did, thank God. I turned back to Caleb urging him to go on.

'Mina. My sources are good, I know you're angry, and I've proper sprung it on you, but I'd rather have 24 hours than nothing. You're the leader here and you have to act fast.'

I let out a frustrated breath that I hadn't realized I was holding and looked at my advisor. I trusted him more than anyone, more than my family that were all seated around the large table of the leader's conference room at St Georges Hall, but I didn't understand a word he'd just said. He wasn't just my Advisor he was my best friend, and he knew I sometimes let my anger control my feelings and, as the leader of the Scouser's Coven, I needed to have a level head.

'OK, OK, tell me everything. Slowly, Caleb. Not that panicked, rambling you've just shouted at me.' I sat down to brace myself and absorb as much information as possible. Caleb also took a long breath and sat beside me, readying himself.

He looked like he might have aged since yesterday, the worry written all over his long, pale face, and his sky-blue eyes narrowed in concentration as he prepared to speak. Just looking at him had me worried. His dark brown hair was messy like he'd been running his hands through it more than usual. And what was he wearing? Caleb always looked smartly dressed but he was in everyday clothes that were crumpled.

'As you know I have sources everywhere,' he began. I nodded, knowing Caleb was very good at finding the right information and had spies everywhere to get it. 'I have already told you that the Newcastle Coven has made moves to conquer the whole country, which we agreed wasn't that great a threat. Well, now I know how they're doing it … They're using dark magic.'

I turned sharply to Caleb and a few gasps came from around the table. Dark magic is forbidden, very powerful, and extremely dangerous, but more importantly it cannot be traced at all. They could move past all the wards I had in place around my city, and I'd have no idea. They would be able to come and go like everyone else in my coven.

I didn't even try to hide my fear and anxiety as I looked around the table at my siblings and cousins, one of whom was heavily pregnant. Bessie, with her long blonde hair down to her knees, and eyes like sparkling emeralds, clutched her stomach in fear as she heard the news. I looked back at Caleb and lifted my chin for him to go on.

'They've gone from Newcastle, right down the coastline, taking Scarborough, then on to York, Hull, and Leeds.' I couldn't believe what I was hearing. No one had ever done this, maybe two covens arguing amongst themselves, but never anyone setting out to conquer more than one city. I had friends in York, the witches there were very friendly and would never want to fight. They would have been easy pickings for the Newcastle army. Caleb spoke again and I winced at what he might say next.

'They crossed the Pennines and took Manchester two weeks ago.'

The shock on my face must have been blatant. Liverpool and Manchester are not what I would call 'besties' but fuck me, it's basically down the road. My family's whispers surrounded me, *'oh my god'*, 'what are we going to do?'

'Mina, they're already here!' Caleb continued. The look I gave him made him cower slightly.

'What do you mean they're here, they can't be! Surely, I would know if they were here!' I was struggling to keep my cool. I was more powerful than most of the cities' Coven leaders, including Newcastle

– my family being one of the original families to grace these lands – and my army was well known to be ruthless. Surely, they would not take that lightly. I had assumed they would go around us and leave us until last.

'Their tactic is to filter their army through the barriers, a few at a time, covered in dark magic, and have them just stay here until they are ready, which my sources say will be tomorrow.'

I frowned in confusion. 'So, you're telling me that the majority of the Newcastle army is just knocking about town right now as we speak, having a pint, going the fucking Wetherspoon? Don't you think we would notice?' No fucking way was I going to believe that.

'It's not that hard of a stretch Mina. Not only are they using dark magic to conceal themselves, but tomorrow the football's on, there's a concert at Liverpool One and every theatre in town has a show on. Tomorrow is most likely one of the busiest days of the year.'

'It's also Chinese New Year tomorrow,' cousin Zayn added.

Realisation dawned on me, every family in the whole of Liverpool would be out in town tomorrow to celebrate everything Liverpool had to offer. The city would already be filling up in preparation. There would be no way to determine if people were coming for other reasons until it was too late. My sister, Cora, looked at me with such fear in her eyes that my heart wanted to break.

'We need to evacuate,' Cora said, gripping the table with her fresh set of acrylic nails. She was still wearing rollers in her hair and a full face of makeup. I stared at the map of Liverpool in front of me and was grateful when Caleb spoke because I didn't think I could attempt to string a sentence together.

'It's too short notice, Cora, and where would we go? Manchester belongs to them now, the next place that is big enough is Wales. How are we getting everyone there before they attack?'

My head was spinning while thinking of all the people that would be around town the next day. I stood and walked to the window, looking out at my city.

Liverpool town centre was beautiful with the sun out, and everyone looking to celebrate the weekend. I could almost hear the children laughing as the Lions and Lambananas chased them, nipping at their feet.

I couldn't 't help but think of the hustle and bustle of people going to work to earn a living. The singers and dancers on the streets, busking to make ends meet. Pete, the old man with blow-up props singing along really badly, and the old man who sits covered in shit and feeds the pigeons. People going to shows and concerts. Liverpool and Everton fans in heavy debates about who plays the best football while enjoying a pint at the bars and clubs. Tourists visiting the museums, cathedrals, and other attractions, and hotels and restaurants jam-packed with happy customers.

Chinese New Year in Liverpool is magical. Giant dragons come to life, dancing through the streets. Celebrations so bright with life, song, and dance that stay with you forever. I couldn't help but think of the beauty of this city, the magic that runs through the streets. Magical waterfalls and statues coming to life. Our giant Liver birds that fly above the buildings always watching over us, protecting us. St Johns beacon shining starlight over the town and the docks every night, docks that have cruise ships and ferries. Our famous Albert dock that I loved to walk through at night. What beauty this city had. What destruction can be made by people with no loyalties to life and love?

I loved this city with everything I had, and I'd sworn to protect it and everyone in it, with my life, and that it is what I would do. Realizing that it was time for me to lead, I was finally ready to act. So, I turned back to the table.

'I'm assuming you have suggestions, Caleb. They better be good.' He straightened like he was prepared for this very conversation.

'Remember when you made the army do drills on how to assemble around the city in emergency situations?'

A small smile grew across my face. 'The ones you deemed a waste of time, and resources?' I asked.

Caleb rolled his eyes. 'Yes, well you were right. We should have our army put out across town in plain clothes. I think we should make subtle changes, so they don't know what's going on. We need to make things happen all at once so they can't react in time. They think we know nothing, let's use that.'

I hated this idea; this idea did not remove the danger to my people. Caleb must have known what I was thinking.

'I know this isn't what you want to hear Mina but it's too late to stop it. We can't flee so we will have to fight.'

I didn't have a problem with fighting, but I did when it was in the middle of my beautiful city, amongst all my people. I had to ask, 'Is this possible though, can we prepare enough in 24 hours? If we fight, can we win Caleb?' I looked into the eyes of the man that had become my main source of strength and pleaded with him to tell me everything would be okay. His sigh, which was filled with so much sadness, was crushing. He took a long deep breath before he spoke.

'I can't tell you this will be easy Mina or that we won't lose anyone, but we have the strongest army in the country and the most powerful leader, so I believe in us. I believe we can do this. Newcastle is an army filled with hate and cruelty. We are a family filled with love and determination, we will not be beaten, Mina.'

I looked around the table at each person in turn, siblings, aunties, uncles, and cousins, knowing what I was silently asking. They knew we had no choice, so each gave me a slight nod in agreement even as their faces filled with fear. I turned to Caleb ready to make the biggest decision of my leadership, the biggest decision of my life. But Caleb was right, so I said it for everyone to understand.

'WE FIGHT!'

Trichotillomaniac
Tashi Thornley

To wake every morning
Guilt ridden from head to toe
You head to the mirror,
Not entirely sure of what will show

Head already spinning of how to cover up
What can be the answer when people ask 'What's up?'

A dare seems the most likely
Followed by drunken prank
Or, be gusty and be truthful
About all the hairs you yank.

It's just not good to look at
When all the face is bare –
Although not as bad as many,
The pulling is still there.

You see a dark root coming
And you want that bastard hair!

The urge – stronger, stronger and stronger
Until finally defeats conceded
That urge you tired to ignore

But eventually you ceded.

Relief is there straight after
Although only fleeting by
Then it really hits you.
The agonising aftermath;
Not just the redness above the eyes,
But the mental state you're left in –
The question of just why?!

Well this is my life, so welcome
Welcome to my life as a
Trichotillomaniac.

I wake every morning
Guilt ridden from head to toe
I head to *my* mirror
Not entirely sure of what will show!

The Smiler
Tashi Thornley

Once known as the smiler,
Her golden shine has gone
The precious life she lived
Is now lost and not won

Her mind is now strangled
On her own thoughts she chokes
But she puts on a show
And she laughs and she jokes.

Inside there's a blackout,
There is no passage through
The warmth has all gone
Now everything is blue.

Nothing now matters,
Not even diamonds or gold
She tries to stay strong
But it's much easier to fold!

Her mind is all foggy
Filled with smoke!

The blood trickles down,
This is no longer a joke.

Rising from the Dark
Tashi Thornley

I've been down for so long
I've been finding it hard to dig my way out
The hole is deeper than ever before
The darkness deafens even my loudest screams and shouts.

'You'll pull through,' so the professionals say
'We know you will – you've been here before,'
But that doesn't make it any easier
When you find yourself knocking on deaths door!

'Let me in! Please let this end.'
You scream as you're knocking on that door
Who don't care who answers – whether from up or down
You just know that you don't have it in you, you can't keep fighting this endless war

But suddenly, I'm rising from dark
This time I tell myself there'll be no more scars
But you've been here before
It's like Groundhog Day – you're always waiting for that fall.

But until that fall comes
Ain't nothing gonna keep me down
I'm hearing the birds sing, the black and white vision has disappeared
Finally my frown had been turned upside down.

My demons have once again been defeated
It's time to recoup my energy stores that are massively depleted
For how long they stay in hiding, I do not know
But while they're gone, I'll ride the high, I'll give life a go!

Because I'm rising from the
I promise myself I have left my last scar
Although the dark nights are closing in,
My brighter days are only just starting to begin.

But here I am, I've done it.
I've risen from the dark like all the times before!
But if that darkness tries to creep back in

Tell yourself this...

Whether you've risen once or a thousand times before,
You have the strength to do it once more.

From the Ashes

Tashi Thornley

A Different Class
Tashi Thornley

Jack Suddington-Smith is 24 from London. His mother is a doctor and his father a politician. Jack has never done a days work in his life and his parents funded him through Eton University in the hope that he might follow in their footsteps. Jack flunked his degree as he spent too much time partying and developed a cocaine habit, he has since ran up reasonable debt from his dealers that he is trying to avoid paying off.

Jack Thomas is 24 from Wavertree in Liverpool He has had a completely different upbringing. He got involved in County Lines when he was 14 and worked his way up the ranks within the gang. He moved to London when he was 20. He has been sent to put Jack in line and demand he pays off his debt.

Jack Suddington-Smith is enjoying an oat latte with a friend in a local coffee shop, bragging to his friend about his wild drug and sex fuelled weekend when in walks Jack Thomas.

Jack Thomas: Jack Suddington-Smith, that's you, ye?
Jack Suddington-Smith: And what's it to do with you may I ask?
JT: It's gotta lot to do with me mate, we need to have a little chat! This your mate, ye?

JSS: Yes actually, it is.

JT: Well, whatever his name is, tell him to do one!

JSS: Well, actually me and Ethan were just in the middle of something.

JT: I won't ask you again lad.

Jack Thomas flashes a glimpse of a gun that is hidden in his jacket.

JSS: *(losing his confident demeanour)* Well, I guess we could always do another time. Ethan, can you leave us be? I'll call you later my friend.

Scrudel Finds a Friend
Tashi Thornley, aged 9

Adam: Good morning boys and girls, what has your day been like? What about you, Scrudel? Scrudel? Scrudel, where are you?
Scrudel: I'm here, hold on a minute, Adam. *(His head pops up)* What where you saying?
Adam: I was saying...what... *(Looks at Scrudel)* ... What's the matter, Scrudel?
Scrudel: Oh, nothing, why do you ask?
Adam: Well, it's just that you look a bit sad, so come on tell me what's wrong.
Scrudel: Well (longingly) I'm bored, that's all.
Adam: Well, why don't you go and play out with your friends?
Scrudel: That's something I was hoping you wouldn't ask, I feel ashamed saying it in front of all these children.
Adam: Well just whisper it to me so the children won't hear you.
Scrudel: Ok then *(whispers)* I haven't got any friends.
Adam: *(loudly)* What, you haven't got any friends?
Scrudel: Hey you said whisper so the children won't hear and then said it dead loudly so they heard it. I hate you. I'm going.
Adam: Hey Scrudel, come back. I didn't mean it *(in the*

distance his voice says no.) Agh, Scrudel ran away, who's going to help me find him?

Tashi comes in with Springu.

Adam: Hi Tashi, what have you been up to?
Tashi: Well, I've got to look after Spring because my sister has gone to Australia for a year. He got bored so I came for a little walk in hopes to find him a friend.
Adam: Well that's great, isn't it boys and girls. You see, my Scrudel needs a friend too. He's been bored all day and has only just told me that he hasn't got any friends either.
Scrudel: *(pops back up)* Here you go again talking about me. You can't ever stop it, no wonder none of your friends like me.
Tashi: Actually, Scrudel, you could never have been more wrong in your life. Adam was just telling me how bored you have been and if there was anything I could do…and, by the way Scrudel, I do like you.
Scrudel: I'm sorry, Tashi. Sorry, Adam. Is there anything you can do?
Tashi: Yes, there is actually. You see that little penguin over there's name is Springy. All you have to do is go over and introduce yourself and then tell him you know me and I'll give him my special wink. Then you you can play with each other and never be bored again.

Scrudel: *(screams)* No! I can't do that. He won't like me, I'll go up to him and he'll laugh in my face and then tell everyone and then I'll never have any friends ever.

Tashi: No, he won't. He's not like that, Scrudel, he's very friendly and will be friends with anyone as long as I give him my special wink.

Adam: Go on, Scrudel. You should be able to trust her by now, you've known her all your life.

Scrudel: Okay, then I'll go over, but if he's horrible I will never speak to you again, either of you.

Scrudel walks over and says hi, and his name and they make friends. Tashi gives her special wink.

Tashi: Well, we have done him good thing. Now he's got loads of confidence and soon he'll have loads of friends.

Scrudel: Thanks a bunch, Tashi. If it wasn't for you, then I would have no friends. Now I'll never be bored again. *(addresses the audience)* So kids, can anyone guess the moral of the story? It is…Never be too shy to make friends, they're more likely to become your friend than be horrible and you never know what you could miss out on.

Springu: Thanks for watching our show! I hope you enjoyed it.

Fly on the Wall
Vincent Quirk

I'm just a fly on the wall, don't look at me
surveyor of all, what do I see
a different class, living like me
love lost and won
pain, hurt, dirt and fun
it's a theatre for you, its life for me
I'm just a fly on the wall
and this is what I see

I'm just a fly on the wall, don't watch me cry
surveyor of all, I can't lie
life is lost, it turns dust
it settles on things and forms a crust
let little things lie, leave them to die
I'm a fly on the wall and I spy

I see things you can't see
it's for the best believe me
you wouldn't like it
it will break your heart
split you in two
it will tear you a part
I'm just a fly on the wall, can you see me now
I'm keeping your secrets; I'm watching you now.

It's All About Love or Lust
Vincent Quirk

Cold friction, damp sheets
Wet hair, soft, supple twisted limbs
Blood like sticky bleach
Used skin with deep cold
Violent, abandoned wasteland
Teeth scraping concrete
Broken bricks on sandpaper skin
Torn flesh at scratching nails
Hollow vomit, dead penetrating splinter
Sweet spit and stagnant foul taste
Decaying panic filled green with sour acidic gagging
Consuming anxiety filled disappointment.

The Extraordinary Story of Glad and Mary
Moon Rice

Where Mary was concerned, boring was best. Boring was comfortable. Boring was no drama and, best of all, boring was cheap. Even as a child, she was boring – so much so that people would sing a song about her. It went:

Mary, Mary, meek and mild
She's never wild
Just sends herself to sleep
She's such a boring child.

This wasn't true of course. Mary never sent herself to sleep but she had done it to others. Taxi drivers refused to take her in case they fell asleep at the wheel and buses and trains made her sit at the opposite end to the driver. There had even been occasions of her boring people to death! On the plus side though, she never got cold callers anymore; no one asking whether she'd found Jesus or asking her to donate to *Save The Decrepit*. So Mary's life wasn't entirely without happiness. One of her chief sources of joy was her goldfish.

Mary's goldfish was Glad. That is to say, Mary's goldfish called themselves Glad. They were not glad to be Mary's goldfish. They hated being Mary's goldfish. In fact, if Glad wasn't so reliant on being fed, they'd really have preferred it if Mary hadn't existed at all.

For a start, Mary insisted on calling Glad, 'Gerald.' Glad would insist they weren't called Gerald – that they weren't even a boy! – but it would get lost in a mass of bubbles every time Glad tried to speak. Mary would also tap on the side of Glad's bowl and coo at them like Glad was an infant rather than the three year old adult they were.

Then 'The Cost of Living Crisis' arrived and this changed things. For some reason, Mary got it into her head that Glad was some kind of performing monkey. It had begun after Mary saw an advert in the paper. It read:

Don't be koi!
Make every fin go swimmingly at
Dr Shubunkin's Golden Goldfishes Training Academy.
I guarantee you'll be bowled over or your money back!

Ever since then, Mary had disappeared every Wednesday at three o'clock and would come back at 5 o'clock with a new trick to show Glad. First there was swimming upside down and then there were the loop-the-loops and then cartwheels. All of these tricks annoyed Glad hugely but tonight was a new low. In the bottom of Glad's bowl was a bicycle.

'What on earth?' Glad wondered. 'She's not thinking I'm gonna ride that, is she? I don't have any feet!'

Unfortunately, this very evident fact hadn't occurred

to Mary as, yes, she did expect Glad to ride the bicycle. Not right away. That would be too much to hope for but, with a few hours practice every day, Mary was sure Glad would eventually get the hang of it.

'Come on, Gerald,' cooed Mary. 'Ride the bicycle. You can do it, little fella!'

Glad swore under their breath. There wasn't enough fish flakes in all the world to make them ride that bicycle! They wouldn't even do it for a new shiny bridge to swim under! There was just no way this was happening! It was like asking a squirrel not to eat nuts or a cat to fetch a stick: it was completely against nature. However, Mary wasn't taking 'no' for an answer and was just getting more and more worked up at Glad's refusal to ride the bicycle. After a few days of this, she relented and bought the optional stabilisers Dr Shubunkin had advised her to buy in the first place. On fitting the stabilisers, Mary could see the improvement at once: no longer would Glad have to pick the bicycle up to ride it. It stood up all by itself.

'Now, come on, Gerald,' said Mary impatiently. 'All you have to do is sit down on that seat and pedal!'

Sadly, however, Mary had done nothing to address Glad's lack of feet with which to pedal. Instead, her focus was on Glad's apparent wilfulness. So, she began to bang on Glad's bowl in frustration.

'Come on, you little fff...ish! I've spent two hundred

pounds on that bike! And it's not like I'm made of money!' Mary shouted at Glad.

Their head banging with all the commotion, Glad was sad and, even though they knew it was no use, they tried to please Mary by lowering themselves onto the bicycle seat. But they couldn't, even if they wanted to, sprout any feet. So, the pedals remained untouched and would not – and could not – move.

This seemed to annoy Mary further and she was now screaming at Glad. This made Glad even sadder and, oh, how they longed to be able to email James Dyson to invent them some ear defenders. Alas they had no more hands than they did feet. So, instead, they went and buried themselves in the pebbles in the bottom of the bowl.

This behaviour made Mary give up in disgust and she began to think she'd never get on *Britain's Got Brilliance* now. She knew full well she was too boring to get on there herself. Besides *The Samaritans* had asked her never to speak in public again after that last time. No. Goldfish training was her ticket to fame and money...except the goldfish wasn't playing ball!

Well, Mary wasn't about to give up. No way, José! Every day she'd try to coax Glad onto the bicycle and every day it'd end in frustration and tempers being lost. Glad was even beginning to think of an escape plan. If only Mary didn't keep them so far from the sink! Then

Mary had an idea.

'That's it!' exclaimed Mary. 'I need to get rid of the water! Asking Gerald to ride the bicycle in water is like me trying to drive in the sea!'

So she plucked Glad and the bicycle with its stabilisers from the bowl and plonked them down on the table.

'Come on, Gerald!' cooed Mary. 'Hop onto your bicycle for me.'

Mary seemed to be completely oblivious to the fact that Glad was wriggling around, gasping for breath.

'Come on, Gerald,' repeated Mary. 'You can do it, little fella.'

Glad was certain this was it. The stupid girl had finally killed them this time. They'd soon be taking that final journey into *The U-Bend of Eternity* from whence no goldfish ever returned. Glad stopped moving and closed their eyes. Suddenly, but, at the same time, slowly, they felt themselves drift away. They were swimming above their body now, in mid-air. Glad could see all the planets sparkling above them and it seemed such a peaceful, magical place, that Glad swam towards them.

Then Glad heard music. It was *Go West* by The Pet Shop Boys and the DJ had faded the music so it was just the choir.

The DJ asked Glad a question in a soft yet firm voice,

'Do you want to live?'

And Glad very much did want to live. So they exclaimed, 'Yes!' as though their life depended upon it…which, of course, it very much did.

So then the DJ asked another question, 'Do you want to live with Mary, Glad?'

Glad didn't even have to think about the answer. They'd very much had their fill of Mary. Not only had she proven to be annoying but also a danger to Glad's life. How could they possibly trust her again? So Glad gave an almost instinctual 'No!' in response.

'In that case, Glad. May I introduce you to Rose,' said the DJ in an amused tone.

And with that, Glad found themselves rushing back into their body as though they were falling down a gigantic waterfall made of stardust. With a little thump that jolted right through their body, they opened their eyes to see a little girl giving them the kiss of life.

'Yuk! Gerroffff!' cried Glad.

Rose was too excited at bringing Glad back to life to pay them any attention. Instead Rose exclaimed, 'Oh wow! My very own goldfish!' and plopped Glad in a jam jar filled with water.

After screeching 'brilliant!' on a seemingly endless loop for a good twenty minutes, Rose began to calm down and think what she'd call her new found goldfish.

Glad was about to tell her that they called themselves 'Glad' because they were so glad to be a goldfish and not some other creature like a hamster or a parrot when the girl exclaimed, 'I know! I'll call you Glad because I'm so very glad to have you in my life!' and, at that point, Glad could not have been happier. This was going to work out just fine.

As for Mary, after flushing Glad down the toilet, she'd given up on her dreams of fame and fortune. She phoned Dr Shubunkin and cancelled the rest of the course. She would get herself a sensible job. It might be boring but at least it would guarantee steady hours with a steady income.

So, on the Wednesday after, instead of heading off to *Dr Shubunkin's Golden Goldfishes Training Academy*, she started her new job at *Smedwick's Fish and Chips* as an Assistant Batterer. There was only one stipulation: she wasn't allowed to talk. Not to anyone.

Desert Island Stuff
Gerard Sheridan

On a desert island all alone; the sound of the waves rolling up and down the shore of white sand with the constant noise of the sea in my ears. The soft white sand beneath my feet as I walk along. It reminds me of a scene from *Robinson Crusoe;* all that was needed was the familiar theme tune from the 70s series. I don't know if anyone still remembers it? I can't think of how long it went on for.

The wind picks up and starts to make the tide much choppier. And noisier. The storm starts to howl around the island, tossing and shaking the palm trees as they bend in the strong and persistent wind.

I discover a book lying there, cast up from the jetsam of the tossing waves. I read the faded title, *Gulliver's Travels* by Johnathan Swift. I felt like an abandoned traveller waiting to be overwhelmed by giants in a foreign land. The waves were certainly bigger now and starting to get intimidating. I just felt small and, well, lost – cast up on a forgotten shore. What other dark and shady creatures lived here? How would I manage to survive being lost here all alone? I don't think there would be any people smaller than me. I was the one who was feeling like a lilliputian among giants. The biggest one of which was this storm that was picking up in tempo. It blew and pounded the island for what seemed like hours, before showing any sign of it moving off somewhere else.

It was Beethoven's *Pastoral Symphony After the Storm* that immediately came to my mind as the whole crescendo of this one started to quieten down. And then complete stillness seemed to prevail over everything on the island and felt like the closest thing to peace that I'd experienced in years. It became so quiet that the silence was deafening. Or seemed to be. Until I could begin to hear the bird life and other animals calling vigorously and happily to one another. The relief after the storm doesn't even begin to describe it. I was just glad to be in one piece – in one piece and now able to enjoy the peace. I thought, 'wouldn't it be great to have a full orchestra play Beethoven's symphony.' But it'll all have to remain in my imagination and head.

The seabirds float effortlessly overhead on the now gently billowing breeze which lifts them and seems to cause them to almost hover in one place for a few moments before they fly on. Some smaller wading birds look for shellfish as they scurry across the sand. The overall experience is one of calm and peacefulness.

I am just now thinking of how I'm going to find a way off this little island of peacefulness; or do I really want to go? I'm not now so sure! I think I quite like it here to tell you the truth. I guess I'll have to try and build a raft, or a canoe. I don't think I fancy swimming away. Not with the prospect of dangerous sharks around the island. Or maybe I'll just hope some ship or other comes to this obscure part of the world.

Read All About It
Ian Tudor

March 6th, 2073
THE GLOBAL
Riots broke out upon the news that gas mask prices would be rising by 30% in the coming months, with protestors claiming that the poor are being priced out of leaving their homes. Demonstrations focused mainly on the factory producing the new generation of gas mask, which claims that although the price is rising, it will mean that users can spend up to 48 hours outside without having to recharge the system. Throughout the course of the protests, gas mask shops and water supply chains were targeted by thieves.

March 9th, 2073
THE STAR NEWS
The Fresh Mountain Water Company once again closed taps over fears about pollution levels in its water. Last week, the company asked customers not to consume the water, and to use only a dampened towel for cleaning themselves. When asked to comment, Fresh Mountain Water declined to put a date on the return to normal service.

April 3rd, 2073
THE POST
Pollution levels have reached an all-time high, as President James Harper promises that the government and its scientists are doing everything they can to stop America following the likes of South Asia and the Persian Gulf in becoming uninhabitable.

April 6th, 2073
THE POST
A lead scientist in the battle of pollution levels today came forward. The scientist wished to stay anonymous, but they did confirm that they have met with the president about the future of Earth. The scientist has warned that it may already be too late to save the planet, as short of a massive breakthrough happening very soon, it could be rendered uninhabitable in as little as four years' time.

April 6th, 2073
THE STAR NEWS
President Harper has spoken out against 'scaremongering,' as he asks for calm following claims made by a whistle-blower scientist regarding the planet's worsening pollution levels. The president stated categorically that the scientist in question is not a member of his official staff, before asking for patience

in the ongoing battle against pollution.

April 9th, 2073
THE PLANET
New water rationing begins this week, with each household only allowed one litre per person. Riots broke out at water supply stations, leading to the army being deployed to deal with protestors. Reports coming from the Midwest, where yesterday a comet crash-landed, describe a crater half a mile wide, with reports claiming that grass is now growing on the once-barren land around the comet.

April 9th, 2073
[Title?]
Dr Amy Woods, a lead scientist in the battle against pollution, today left her position at the Whitehouse. Dr Woods told the assembled press that she wishes to spend more time with her family after her husband was injured in a car accident, before offering reassurances that the government is working hard behind the scenes and stating her belief that a solution is close to being found.

May 23rd, 2073
THE GLOBAL
As wildfires burn throughout the country, NASA says

that a comet will fly close by the planet in the coming weeks.

June 3rd, 2073
THE PLANET
NASA scientists are worried that a comet which had been due to fly past earth in the coming weeks has changed trajectory and is now on a collision course with the planet.

June 23rd, 2073
THE GLOBAL
With news of the approaching comet spreading, the world was plunged into chaos. People scrambled to prepare for the worst, stocking up on whatever food, water, and supplies they could find, while others gathered with loved ones to wait out the impending disaster. As the days passed, the comet grew larger in the dusty, red polluted sky, its tail stretching across the horizon like a fiery dragon's breath. The world held its breath as the comet drew nearer and nearer, and scientists scrambled to calculate the exact time and location of the impact.

Finally, the day arrived. People huddled in shelters or stood outside, watching the sky in awe and terror as the comet hurtled towards Earth. Some prayed for a miracle, while others resigned themselves to their fate.

But as the comet drew closer, something miraculous happened. It began to slow down and break up, and as it flashed through the dusty sky somewhere over the Midwest, eyewitnesses reported that, for a second, the sky turned blue and the polluted air seemed clearer.

June 24th, 2073
THE GLOBAL
Reports coming from the Midwest, where the comet crash-landed yesterday, say there is a crater half a mile wide. We are hearing reports that grass is growing on the barren land around the comet.

June 25th, 2073
THE GLOBAL
Reporter Gary Owens is at the scene where the meteor crashed. The government have now taken over the site and are asking people to avoid the area. Eyewitness reports say that the government arrived soon after the meteor touched down and immediately set up a cordon. People in the area reported that grass was growing at the site and the air was breathable and clean. Government officials have been reached out to, but we have had no reply as yet.

June 26th, 2073
THE GLOBAL
Still no reports coming out of the meteor crash site, where large trucks and various scientists have been seen entering in large numbers.

June 27th, 2073
THE POST
President Harper has today been to visit the site of the meteor crash. He and his staff were present on the ground for around four hours, with a briefing is scheduled for tomorrow afternoon.

June 28th, 2073
THE STAR
President Harper addressed the nation today on the matter of the comet crash, during which he confirmed earlier reports of grass growing and air pollution dropping drastically at the site. Scientists are now studying the meteor, hoping to discover a way to replicate its effects on the environment around the world. The President also stated that NASA is working to track where the meteor originated from, in the hope that more of them could perhaps be discovered in space.

July 2nd, 2073
THE GLOBAL
President Harper again addressed the nation today, along with the head of NASA Greg Sullivan and lead scientist Dr Lisa Briggs. Sullivan says NASA has traced the comet back to a small planet just outside the solar system, and is now looking at ways to develop a craft to travel there using hyper-drive and worm holes to hopefully reach its destination within two years.

Dr Briggs has said that with pollution around the meteor at zero levels, the grass is growing, the air is breathable, and the water from a nearby lake is drinkable. Dr Briggs puts this down to minerals found inside the meteor, with efforts already under way to attempt to replicate these minerals.

Trees
Keith Anthony Vaughan

Trees rustling in the wind
on a dull autumn day

The fine summer sunshine
has become a distant memory

The branches of the trees sway
back and forth

The trees' dispositions
have changed from such greenery
In the summer months,
to unpleasant brownish amber
colour with leaves ready
to fall individually to the ground

Trees are so prevalent
in their domain, and it is such a
characteristic part of nature
in the countryside and forest.

Afterword

Congratulations to all those who participated in Write to Work, for producing such high-quality writing for *From the Ashes*, and being generous enough to share their stories with us.

Writing on the Wall is a dynamic Liverpool-based community organisation, which celebrates writing in all its forms. We hold two annual festivals and a series of year-round projects, working with a broad and inclusive definition of writing that embraces literature, creative writing, journalism and non-fiction, poetry, songwriting, and storytelling. We work with local, national and international writers whose work provokes controversy and debate, engaging in all of Liverpool's many diverse communities in order to promote and celebrate both individual and collective creativity.

If you have a story to tell and would like to take part in one of our writing projects, or perhaps work with us to develop a new initiative, please do get in touch. We'd love to hear from you.

Madeline Heneghan and Mike Morris
Co-Directors

MORE BOOKS FROM WRITING ON THE WALL

writingonthewall.org.uk/shop